Herbert Hiram Hayden

The Rev. Herbert H. Hayden

An Autobiography

Herbert Hiram Hayden

The Rev. Herbert H. Hayden
An Autobiography

ISBN/EAN: 9783337116057

Printed in Europe, USA, Canada, Australia, Japan

Cover: Foto ©Raphael Reischuk / pixelio.de

More available books at **www.hansebooks.com**

THE

Rev. Herbert H. Hayden

AN

AUTOBIOGRAPHY

THE

Mary Stannard Murder

TRIED ON CIRCUMSTANTIAL EVIDENCE

———

ILLUSTRATED

HARTFORD
PRESS OF THE PLIMPTON MFG. CO.
1880

CONTENTS.

THE REV. HERBERT H. HAYDEN.

[From a photograph taken Dec., 1879.]

INTRODUCTION.

THE trial of the Rev. Herbert H. Hayden, of Madison, Conn., on a charge of murdering Mary Stannard, was begun in New Haven on the 7th of October, 1879, and was not concluded till near the middle of January, and, considering the time occupied, the character of the evidence and other circumstances, it was one of the most memorable trials in the court annals of this country. Public interest in it became absorbed from the start ; and the wide-spread knowledge of it and watchful curiosity to learn every phase of it have been strikingly illustrated in the overwhelming correspondence that the publishers of this book have received from one end of the country to the other, making inquiries concerning the sale and price of the work.

Readers will find in the testimony of Mr. and Mrs. Hayden, and in the abstracts of the arguments of counsel, a record of the leading events in the trial, together with the essential features of testimony which formed the scheme of the prosecution and the defensive elements on the other side. It has not been considered necessary to follow in detail the whole mass of evidence, material or speculative, which occupied the attention of the State throughout, because very much was introduced manifestly in support of theories which were finally not pressed. A sufficiently comprehensive idea of the leading facts and material elements of the trial is given to satisfy all readers—even those who have not pursued with care the current record of the proceedings.

Mr. Hayden himself, from the start, maintained a calm faith in the final result of the trial. He was never demonstrative, but always self-assured and confident. As an example of this, the following partial report of a conversation had with him in the New Haven jail while the trial was in progress, and before the defence had been heard, is given :

Mr. Hayden was asked if he should testify in his own behalf, and he replied : "I certainly expect to."

Question—"You testified, I believe, at the hearing before Justice Wilcox at South Madison in September, 1878 ?"

Answer—"I did."

Question—"Will your testimony be given substantially as it was then ?"

Answer—"Of course it will. What was true then is true now."

Question—"If you do not care to go over the grounds of that testimony here, may I ask you what your feeling is with reference to the result of the present trial ?"

Answer—"I have perfect confidence in the intelligence and fairness of the twelve men who are to pass upon the case, and have no fears as to the result."

Question—"Of course you must feel in your situation considerable anxiety, or at least occasionally some degree of nervousness or impatience over the position you are in ?"

Answer—"Certainly. The deprivation of a man's liberty is, under any and all circumstances, oppressive, and I have felt keenly the embarrassment of my position at times ; but there has never been a moment when I have had any fear of my final vindication."

Question—"In the progress of the trial there have been some striking points, such as the abandonment of various theories, manifestly considered of some importance by the attorneys for the State, which have certainly turned public opinion strongly upon your side, and you must have watched them with considerable interest ?"

Answer—"I have probably felt less interest in them, than the public has, because from their very inception I knew there was no foundation for them. I feel, however, that these various matters which the State has from time to time adhered to and then abandoned are all greatly to my advantage."

It was while in jail that Mr. Hayden, upon the advice of friends, conceived the idea of writing his Autobiography, with reference to the publication of a book concerning the trial, out of the sale of which he might derive something toward liquidating the heavy obligations incurred in his defence, besides getting means of support for his family—himself, wife and three children. His life has been a hard struggle, as all will admit who read the story of his exertions to educate himself and do a good work in the world ; and the noble devotion of his wife in assisting him to accomplish his well-directed efforts, shows what that struggle was, and how much of self-sacrifice there was in his life and what burdens he and his devoted wife jointly bore. He had but just become established in a field where he was able, by constant labor, to provide a comfortable living for his family—and only just able. The work he had to do was surprisingly great. Only those who have had the trials of a country clergyman's place in a small parish can realize how much work must be done to keep soul and body together.

In the midst of these trials and struggles he was taken on the terrible charge of murder. He was kept in jail for nearly fourteen months before his trial began. With no means of support, except such as kind friends might furnish, his family was dependent ; but there were Christian homes ready to receive the suffering wife and children, and this provision for their comfort and care was a great relief to the imprisoned husband. But there were expenses to be borne of great magnitude—greater than was at first anticipated, by reason of the prolonged length of the trial—and to aid in the cancellation of these is a motive which strongly governs Mr. Hayden in the effort he now makes to derive an income and replenish his empty purse.

Mr. Amos Cummings, a well-known journalist, who attended the trial, prepared the following, which was published in the New York *Sun*. It is given here for its general interest, and to show how an impartial writer viewed the scenes and incidents of the trial :

The prosecution have examined one hundred and six witnesses, and the defense seventy. In this array of witnesses Mrs. Hayden stands the central figure. Her beauty, modest demeanor and positive language place her on the highest pedestal. Clad in a close-fitting black dress that showed the symmetry of her form to perfection, she stood like a statue with uplifted hands while the oath was administered. For two days she retained remarkable self-possession, and broke into tears only when Mr. Waller subjected her to the terrible ordeal that drew upon him the indignation of those whose sympathies are possibly untempered by the best of judgment. The appearance of Susan Hawley, the half sister of the murdered girl, presented a marked contrast to that of Mrs. Hayden. Poor Susan's toilet was not in the best of taste. Her complexion was sallow, and her small, gray eyes lacked the magnetism of the expressive brown orbs of the clergyman's wife. One was a cultivated woman, and the other an untutored country girl. Susan burst into tears under the pressure of a courteous but persistent cross-examination; Mrs. Hayden wept because Mr. Waller's pointed interrogatories touched her to the soul. One wept from annoyance, the other from pain. Susan was vacillating and hesitating, and at times refused to answer annoying questions; Mrs. Hayden answered all questions promptly, fluently and grammatically. Susan Hawley appeared on the stand five days, and Mrs. Hayden three.

Among the witnesses were twelve distinguished professors. Eight were from Yale College. These eight were headed by Professor Edward S. Dana, who occupied the witness stand five days. Scientific blood coursed through his veins from the hour of his birth. His mother is a Silliman, and his father a distinguished savan. By right of birth alone he might lay claim to a seat in the

House of Lords of Yale College. On the witness stand he displayed the bearing and breeding of a scientific aristocrat. This was apparently done unconsciously, and was probably due to a combination of conscious knowledge and youthful zeal. An unfortunate slip of the tongue at the beginning of his long cross-examination often returned to plague him. In answer to a question concerning the microscopic measurements of arsenical octahedrons, under the spur of a deft suggestion by his inquisitor, he said there was something about it that "no ordinary mortal could understand." This expression was flung into the faces of other professors called by the prosecution. It served as a sort of a scarlet banner to excite a gilt-horned savan when all other means failed. Prof. Dana's answers were clothed in a redundancy of adjectives. He never used a word of one syllable when one of five would answer the purpose. His explanations were mostly composed of Latin and Greek derivatives strung on a scarcely distinguishable Anglo-Saxon thread. Robin Hood's barn was brought into frequent play, and the route was occasionally so sinuous that the professors lost their way, returned to the original starting point, and took up the trail anew. Despite these facilities of inexpression, Prof. Dana's testimony was of the utmost interest and importance. He is probably the first man in this country who has described the manufacture of arsenic.

Profs. Wm. Henry Brewer, of Yale, and Theodore G. Wormley, of Philadelphia, were more felicitous in their explanations than Mr. Dana. They are veterans in the ranks of science. Abstruse scientific points were made so plain that a boot-black could understand them. The lawyers caught them in no traps. Every pit-fall was avoided, and the professors came out of the fog of cross-examination with clear throats and sound lungs. Not so, however, with Prof. Moses C. White. A more conscientious witness never stood before a jury. He was so conscientious that if asked if he had seen a certain object, he would qualify his answer by saying that his eyes saw it.

"Will you swear that your eyes saw it?" his tormentor would shout.

"I will swear that they saw it to the best of my knowledge and belief," the professor would cautiously respond.

"Will you swear that there is not the shadow of a possibility that your eyes may have been mistaken?"

"I will swear, to the best of my knowledge and belief, that I do not think they were mistaken," the professor would reply.

"Will you swear, to the best of your knowledge and belief, that there is not a shadow of a possibility that they *may* have been mistaken? Come, sir; yes or no," persisted his interlocutor.

"I cannot give a positive answer," the professor would say.

Then the lawyers would kick up a dust, causing the jury to either lose sight of the professor entirely, or to catch no more than a glimpse of his meaning.

Worst of all, Prof. White, after a superficial examination of a stone found near the body of Mary Stannard, had expressed the opinion at the preliminary examination in Madison that it was stained with blood. He had counted and measured some of the corpuscles. After his examination, and before his appearance at the trial in New Haven, he discovered that the stain was a moss or lichen known as algæ. Mr. Watrous, of counsel for defense, forced him to make a public acknowledgment of his mistake. Nor did he rest satisfied with this acknowledgment. Prof. White was called by the prosecution six different times to testify to matters of scientific import. First, it was concerning the arsenic; next, the condition of Mary Stannard's stomach; then the gash in the throat; anon, the blood, pumpkin and pear stains on the various knives thrown into the case; after that the ovarian outgrowth; and, finally, concerning evidences of maternity. In each case the algæ, jumping back, was set in motion, to the confusion of the prosecution and the demoralization of the rigidly conscientious professor. He feebly parried the thrusts. At times Mr. Waller would run to his defence with an argumentative claymore, but he was invariably driven to cover and the effect of the professor's testimony deadened.

Dr. Joshua B. Treadwell, of Boston, was one of the most remarkable of the expert witnesses. He was a sharp-featured man, with piercing black eyes and a tendency to baldness. He wore a soft, wide-awake hat, with a black band twice the width of its rim. He was positive in his assertions, and aggressive toward all who did not agree with him. Mr. Watrous annoyed him as a yellow-jacket would annoy a mettlesome colt. The Boston expert would snort and cavort until his foot was caught in his breeching, when he would kick himself loose and start off at full speed, with all the lawyers after him, the defence trying to keep him going and the prosecution to lariat him. At one time he became so involved that he was unable to do a sum in simple division. In one of his tantrums he kicked Prof. Joseph J. Woodward, of Washington, who gladly accepted an invitation from the defence to come to New Haven and kick back. Woodward was a marvel. He talked as though fed with words from a steam engine. The lawyers were frequently unable to stop his tongue, and at times he himself seemed unable to stop it. The hobby of both these experts was blood corpuscles. The Boston man was certain that he could restore the dried corpuscles, and then determine whether they were the corpuscles of human or animal blood, and the Washington man was equally positive that he could not. To thoroughly appreciate the merits of the dispute, the reader should take into account the amount of blood discovered. Take all the corpuscles said to have been found on the Hayden knife and shirt, and they would make a drop of blood 4,999,999 times smaller than this degree mark ($^{\circ}$).

Fifteen doctors appeared among the witnesses. They were of all grades and shapes, from the burly, red-faced country doctor, who travels the highway laden with calomel and Dover's powders, to the ornate, white-handed city physician, who talks learnedly of hypodermic injections and hydrate of chloral. The profession, however,

maintained its old-time reputation—none of the doctors agreed.
Dr. White swore that he found an outgrowth on the left ovary ; Dr.
Jewett was positive that it was on the right ; a third doctor made an
examination and saw no outgrowth ; and old Dr. Matthewson
seemed to be in doubt as to the existence of either an outgrowth or
an ovary. The lines were equally drawn as to the effect of such an
outgrowth. All the doctors for the defence were of the opinion that
it could produce no symptoms of maternity, and those called by the
prosecution were equally as positive that it would produce such
symptoms. There was the same trouble over the stomach. About
a quarter of the physicians seemed to think that arsenic, whether
taken into a dead or live stomach, would produce symptoms of
inflammation ; others thought not ; others opined that it might do so
if taken into a live stomach, but not if taken into a dead one, and
vice versa. All the doctors looked wise. Young practitioners hardly
out of their medical swaddling clothes were among them, and their
efforts to look as wise as their seniors were instructive and
entertaining.

The diagrams drawn by the doctors were not the least
interesting feature of the medical testimony. A score of œsopha-
guses, pericardiums and similar organs were penciled and laid before
the jury. They were wonderfully and fearfully made. Any
common man might have mistaken them for drawings of Edison's
electric light ; but the jury examined them with great patience, and
seemed to get an inkling of their meaning.

Four Methodist Episcopal clergymen were among the witnesses.
All were contradicted in important particulars by members of their
own churches. Mr. Hayden was the most prominent of these
ministers. He answered all questions promptly, qualifying many
critical replies with reservations. His cross-examination was severe
and persistent, but he never lost his temper. His face would flush
under insinuative questions, and his eyes flash, but his replies were
soft and plaintive. At certain points Mr. Hayden leaned forward

in the box, apparently to give emphasis to particular portions of his testimony. This done, he resumed his usual easy position, with his legs crossed and his right arm swung over the back of his chair. Once he persisted in making an explanation of an apparent contra- diction of his testimony in the preliminary examination at Madison. Again, he refused to give an answer that he thought would place him in a false position, but, at the request of his counsel, he finally answered the inquiry in the trust that Mr. Jones would set him right on the re-direct examination. He was on the stand three whole days and a part of the fourth day. The Rev. Richard S. Eldridge, who contradicted both Mr. and Mrs. Hayden on a mate- rial point of evidence, is pale and intellectual. He has soft black eyes and a soft manner. His wife, whose testimony confirmed his recollections, was lady-like and attractive. The Rev. Joseph Wilbur Gibbs, the pastor of the Rockland Methodist Episcopal church in Rockland, also contradicted Mrs. Hayden and members of his church on important issues. He is large-boned, rough and ready in manner, and equally at home behind the plow or the pulpit. His testimony seemed to excite the indignation of both Mr. and Mrs. Hayden. Mr. Eldridge's testimony apparently pained them, and they intimated that they thought he was honestly mistaken. So much for the ethical testimony.

The hard-fisted Rocklanders were the meat, bone and sinew of the case. Many were unsophisticated, but hard-headed. Such stood the perils of a cross-examination without flinching. Others were nonchalantly self-confident. These retired from the stand with lowered crests. Some promptly answered questions that they did not understand ; others responded before questions were fully put, and a few refused to make a direct answer to any question. There were some startling contradictions indicative of perjury. Old Ben Stevens towered above all the Rockland witnesses. Apparently standing on the brink of the grave, with hollow cheek and sunken eye, he used strong and idiomatic language in repelling insinuative

inquiries, and at times hovered on the border of profanity.   His
remark that he would not converse with two old neighbors over the
murder, "because he did not want to expose" himself, created a
profound impression, which was not entirely removed by his subse-
quent assertion that its purport was misconstrued.   His bearing
was defiant, in marked contrast to the timid manner of the father
of the murdered girl, who burst into tears while describing his
search in the wood and his discovery of the body.

The trial has been nearly devoid of humorous scenes.   One,
however, can never be forgotten by those who saw it.   It is that of
the statuesque deaf woman, who sat five hours with a japanned
trumpet to her ear.   Jones and Waller stood over her shouting in
the trumpet and gesticulating until the veins on their foreheads were
distended and their temples throbbed.   The old lady, however,
heard no more than she wanted to hear, and answered all queries in
a mild voice and an immobile manner.   All the cross-examination
failed to shake her statement that, when she saw a pair of breeches
moving, she was satisfied that there was a man inside of them.

MR. HAYDEN, MRS. HAYDEN AND THEIR CHILDREN

AUTOBIOGRAPHY.

IN the year 1850, in Taunton, Mass., while the nation was
celebrating the anniversary of its first President, I first saw the
light.

At the time of my birth my father's family consisted of himself,
wife, and two children, both boys. Since then a daughter has been
added. Death never has entered the household, and the family
circle in this respect remains unbroken.

My parents were hard-working people—my father being a
shoemaker by trade. When I was one and a half years old my
father secured the position of toll-gatherer of what was then called
the Berkley Draw-Bridge, a responsible but not a lucrative
position. When I was four years of age my father moved to
Dighton, Mass., where he opened a country store and drove a
flourishing trade for many years.

The town of Dighton is beautifully situated on the left bank of
the Taunton river, about ten miles from its mouth. At the time
of which I speak there was carried on a flourishing commercial
trade; so that, at times, there was shipping from all parts of the
coast. There was also a large woollen mill, a rolling mill, and a
tack factory, all of which were in full operation and brought into
the place more or less of a foreign population. In this place I
spent all of my boyhood days; attending the village school, working
in the store and tack factory, and occasionally sailing along the
Middle and New England coast.

Among the earliest of my recollections is an event which indelibly impressed itself upon my memory, and the result of which I shall carry to the grave. When I was four years old it was decided that I should attend the district school. So one bright summer's morning, with my new primer under my arm, I arrived at the schoolhouse in time to join the children at play. While we were playing, and before the teacher had come, by some means I managed to fall. Now, it's an easy thing to fall; and but little injury follows, if you fall in the right place and in the right way. But never was I so fortunate as to fill these two conditions. At this time I fell, striking my face upon the sharp edge of a desk, driving my teeth through my under lip, and cutting my tongue so that it held by a mere shred.

School was over, for me, that day. The doctor was called, and after stitching my tongue and blaming me for my carelessness, I was left to reflect for the first time upon the perils which attend the human race. This event, at the very beginning of my school life, was not encouraging and might have seemed ominous of evil; but, like a certain Roman Consul, disregarding all omens (when he threw the sacred geese into the sea), I pressed on; but, like the Consul, pressed on to defeat!

There are certain incidents in boyhood life, small in themselves, that go a long way in making up the man. They mould and fashion the habits of thought and action after long years have passed away. When I was ten years of age an incident happened to me which I dare say never occurred to any other boy in the land. It was small in and of itself, but its influence was such that it remains to this day, and I can never forget the other actor in this little drama. The incident is unlike those which John B. Gough narrates as occurring in his life—namely, the pulling off of the old man's wig; or, in later years, the passing of the spittoon in the Advent meeting for the purpose of taking a collection for ascension robes; though mine, like his, occurred within sacred walls.

I had been in the habit of accompanying my parents to one of the village churches, there being two in the place. It was a matter of compulsion ; for, unlike Samuel, I made not the sanctuary my choice. On one Sunday while the minister was deeply involved in unfolding the Calvinistic doctrine of predestination, according to the Divine decree before the foundation of the world, and the congregation was wrapt in profound and undivided attention, I, by another decree, was making considerable noise in turning the leaves of a Sunday school picture-book. I naturally thought that these two decrees were all that existed with reference to that day and congregation. Mark my surprise and consternation when suddenly I was apprised of another. I was, without warning, lifted high in the air and bodily carried to a remote corner of the church and seated harshly.

This event made so deep and lasting an impression upon me that ever since, Jonah like, I have shunned all Calvinistic decrees.

At the age of sixteen years I was apprenticed to learn the carpenter's trade, receiving one dollar per day for the first year. Being somewhat proficient at the work, at the end of two years I received journeyman's wages, which at that time was three dollars a day.

When in my eighteenth year, an event occurred which was destined to change the whole course of my life. I had entered upon my chosen profession—a profession selected after long and careful consideration—and in which success crowned my every effort, when the finger of destiny pointed to another field of duty, and a voice said : " This is the way : walk ye in it."

I had been a light-hearted, easy-going youth, apparently beloved by all with whom I came in contact. Worldly I was, it is true, but never descending into paths of sin and degredation, such as are trodden by many of the young at the present day. I do not want to be understood as saying that I was like the elder son, who never strayed from the father's house, or that it was always easier for me to do right than to do evil, for long since my experience has been summed up in the words of Paul: "When I would do good, evil is ever present with me."

I need not stop here to describe the circumstances of my conversion. Suffice it to say that I was an unwilling subject. I fought against it; I prayed against it. I even defied Heaven to gain access to my heart; but it was against the Mighty One that I waged this unequal contest—the creature with the Creator; and, Goliah as I was, I was slain in the presence of Israel.

The taking of Jerusalem by Titus is a fitting illustration of the manner in which my conversion took place. First, the outer walls were carried; then the inside intrenchments; and last of all the citadel itself.

Thus, in my case, the fear of man—the outer walls—was overcome; then the scruples of making a public profession were conquered—these were the inside intrenchments; and, last of all, my tendency to worldly pleasures and ornaments was subdued, and the citadel, the heart itself, belonged to the Conqueror.

But, although I had yielded my heart, the struggle with the unseen Power was not ended. I soon found myself in the midst of a fierce (so far as it related to me) contest as to my future field of duty. No sooner had I been brought to light and liberty than the voice said: "Henceforth, go, work in my vineyard!"

I had no idea of yielding to this work. I had always avoided the different ministers of the place. Not that I disliked them personally, but the life of a minister was distasteful to me. The idea of being servant to all men; of being found fault with on all occasions; of being poorly paid; of having one's best and noblest efforts distorted and drawn out of all recognizable shape, was at war with the spirit of independence within me.

"He is a friend to publicans and sinners," was often said when Christ was on earth. I have found in a minister's life that to be such a friend in the zealous work of unselfish love and devotion to the cause of the Master is to run the risk of losing reputation and friends. The moment a minister of the gospel seeks to raise the fallen of humanity, that moment the hearts of many in his church and congregation are closed against him. This is a broad statement, but in the main it is true. I had seen enough in my short life to infer many of the difficulties of the ministry. It is at its easiest and best a life of toil and heavy burdens. I cannot conceive but that it is the duty of the minister to seek and to save the lost ; to seek in cellars and garrets ; in dens where vice and sin abound— outcasts of society, who otherwise would never hear the "good tidings of great joy" to them ; to save even the prodigal living upon the husks. Knowing this to be the minister's work, and knowing, also, the support generally given to him while engaged in it, and the base and false accusations often coming open-handed from all sides, I shrank from entering such a field of duty. But the more I shrank from it, the more I fought against it, the more I determined not to yield, the stronger the spirit strove; and the Angel seemed more determined to stay.

Having this constant battle to fight, I became very uneasy and disturbed. A change came over my feelings and all my actions. I no longer was a light and merry-hearted youth, but was heart-stricken, sore, weary and depressed. The minister sent for me and inquired into the cause of my trouble. "Trouble," said I, " I have no trouble. I have good health, plenty of work, good pay and hosts of friends ! What more could one desire ?"

With a knowing look he said : "Beware how you tempt Providence ; for God's spirit will not always strive with man."

I appeared as indifferent as possible, though I began to feel my determination giving way. Said the minister, looking me squarely in the face: "You feel it your duty to preach the gospel ; you cannot deceive me. I have been through the same hard struggle. Yield to Him who says 'I will guide thee with mine eye.'"

I took my hat and rushed from the house, without once telling him whether he was right or wrong. Up to this time I had not spoken to a living soul of the struggle within me. My parents, my friends, my minister—all had noticed the change and anxiously awaited the result.

I determined to leave the place. I sought and found work in Mansfield, Mass., a place in which I was a perfect stranger. The same struggle continued—the same resistance prevailed. I had been in Mansfield but a fortnight, had attended but two or three meetings, when a note was placed in my hands. It was from an influential man in the place. Reading the note I found but a single request: "Please call on me tomorrow evening; I wish to converse with you." I thought it strange, but, nevertheless, went at the appointed time. On arriving at the house I was shown into the owner's private room, and immediately was joined by him in person. He opened the conversation by saying : " Ever since you have been in the place, I have noticed that you are having a severe inward struggle." He then asked : " How long have you been converted ?" I told him about eight months. He then said : "You are called to the ministry and don't wish to enter it."

I was taken wholly off my guard. I was comparatively a stranger in the place, and thought my burden was known only to me and my God. But now in my own place a Methodist—and here a Congregationalist—had truthfully told me the cause of all my trouble and sorrow.

What could I do? Where should I go? Do you wonder that I compared myself to Jonah when he was called to go to Nineveh?

I unburdened my heart to this stranger. I told him all my long, fierce struggle; I showed him my poor, wounded, broken spirit; and when, a little later, I went and told Jesus, the burden was removed. I had grace to say :

> " I yield, I yield ; I can hold out no more !
> I sink, by dying love compelled,
> And own Thee conqueror."

The struggle over, the burden removed, my buoyant spirits returned, and life once more seemed worth the living. I immediately began my preparation for the ministry.

In the fall of 1869 I entered the Providence Conference Seminary at East Greenwich, R. I., expecting, as I afterwards did, to work my way through the school. Having once entered upon the work, I had no thought of abandoning it. I taught school; I worked at my trade; I sold books; I worked on the farm; I preached on Sunday. I was happy because I was doing all that I could for the Master. Two years of school life had passed away—two years of hard, earnest work; two years of sound, solid comfort.

I had previously planned at this time to change my condition in life. I was betrothed to Miss Rosa C. Shaw, of Carver, Mass. At this time she was a successful school teacher in Fall River, Mass. Within one year she had lost mother, brother and sister—all of whom died of consumption. These bereavements had so worked upon her that apparently she was about to follow them. The doctor gave her but one year to live. A change of scene, a different relation in life, might avail.

We were married August 8th, 1871, in Plymouth, Mass. We immediately went to housekeeping in East Greenwich. During the winter of 1871–2 we both taught school, my wife nobly endeavoring to carry a part of the burdens of living. During the next summer vacation our first child, a daughter, was born. In the spring of 1873 I completed my course at the seminary, and entered college at Middletown, Conn. After passing my examination I went to Martha's Vineyard, Mass., to work during the vacation.

While here I had my first serious sickness. I was stricken down with typhoid fever, and my life for days hung in the balance. At last I rallied and returned to Middletown. In doing this I made a serious mistake; for, beginning work before I was really strong, I brought on a trouble with my head, and was compelled to abandon the fall term at school.

Determined not to lose too much ground, I, against all advice, kept up a course of reading at my home. At this time my wife was keeping a club of twelve boarders of my own class. This supported us, and removed a heavy burden from our minds.

During the winter term I attended school and made considerable progress. I was straining every nerve, but working under difficulties. I felt that sooner or later I must again stop. When the spring term came I was again overdone and compelled to stop.

One year of college life had gone, and I had accomplished but little in the college course; still I was not wholly disheartened. I secured work at my trade during the vacation. I kept in the open air, and began to amend. I took fresh courage, and entered college in the fall with a determination to retrieve my lost ground.

Again I had to yield. I secured a position in West Rocky Hill to preach on the Sabbath, and left school for the term. During the winter term I again made considerable progress. It was during this term, in December, that our second child, a boy, was born.

I again entered school in the spring term, but was compelled to stop soon after. Thus two years of college life had passed, and out of six terms I had put in but two terms. I thought it best to stop altogether, and accordingly in the spring of 1875 we moved to West Rocky Hill, where I had been preaching for some time.

The people gave us a warm reception, and the year we spent in that place gave us undivided pleasure.

FIRST GOES TO ROCKLAND.

In the spring of 1876 I was appointed to a place called
Rockland, by the Presiding Elder of the district. I went to supply
the next Sabbath, and found the minister, who had preached there
for two years, had not been notified of his removal. I called a
meeting of the stewards, and notified them of my intention not to
come to them, though I had been regularly appointed. They
wanted time for consideration, and also wished to hear me preach.

I therefore preached on Sunday to them, and in the stewards'
meeting it was unanimously decided that I must remain. In May I
removed my family to Rockland, and spent a prosperous year with
that people.

The next year, 1877, I had determined to cease from ministerial
labor and recruit my strength by work in the open air. W. C.
Blakeman was appointed by the conference to supply Rockland.

I secured a small farm, and entered upon my new work. Every
day I felt my strength returning, and in a few months I was
comparatively a new man.

In August, 1877, I was waited upon one Saturday afternoon by a
man from Madison, who desired me to supply the Methodist pulpit
the following Sabbath, as their pastor was sick. I went, and at the
close of the service was waited upon by the stewards, with the

request that I should preach for them until their pastor's health was restored.

I cared not to enter the regular work until the next spring, and thinking that this would be work only for a few weeks, I consented to go.

Soon I found out that I had entrapped myself. The pastor's health did not improve, and the stewards would not let me go. I found myself actively engaged in the work of the ministry, in a field of labor ten miles from home. I accordingly worked on my farm during the week, and on Sunday rode ten miles, preached two sermons, attended Sunday school, and led the evening prayer-meeting.

During the winter I secured a school to teach at the place where I was preaching. This winter—the winter of 1877-8—was the first time that I was separated from my family in all our married life. I would leave home on Saturday, preach on Sunday, teach all the week, and return home Friday night.

My wife felt that she could not stay at home alone nights; and, as she was to teach the school in the place where we lived, we decided that it was best to hire help. Accordingly Mary E. Stannard was employed to come Saturday afternoon and stay until Friday evening, when I returned home.

This state of affairs lasted until the end of February, 1878, when my wife's school closed. A month later my school closed, and I returned to my family.

In April, 1878, I was regularly appointed to preach at Madison. I had come to love the people both of the church and congregation; and as they earnestly desired me to remain with them, I consented to, with the understanding that I could work on my farm and teach during the winter if I felt disposed.

During the early part of 1878 things went smoothly. Putting my heart in the work and my shoulder to the wheel, I was content with the portion allotted to me.

During August of this year our third child, a daughter, was born. My wife was recovering rapidly, and insisted that I should pay my parents a visit.

I left home the 19th of August, with the understanding that I should be absent as long as desirable. I returned, however, a week from the next Monday. I preached the following Sabbath at Madison. This was on the 1st of September, 1878. The following Friday, the 6th of September, I found myself a prisoner in the harsh hands of the law, charged with the murder of Mary E. Stannard, who seven months before had worked in my family while I was teaching ten miles away.

I have stated that I preached at Madison the preceding Sabbath. I returned home on Monday, and on Tuesday, about sunset, I was notified that Mary E. Stannard had been found with her throat cut up in the Brag lots.

I immediately went to the scene of the homicide, and assisted in removing the body to the house; rode half the night for a jury of inquest; testified when called the next afternoon, and toward night was told that I was suspected of being the perpetrator of the crime. .

Had the earth opened at my feet I could not have been more surprised. To think that, after all I had done for the poor, unfortunate girl and her father's family, they should entertain such a thought, was enough to drive me mad.

All through that long, dreary night the terrible ordeal through which I must shortly pass haunted me. Sleep deserted me. I tried to pray; but all that I could say was: "My God! my God! Why hast Thou forsaken me?"

My wife lay sweetly sleeping by my side, with the three weeks' old babe upon her breast. I had purposely refrained from telling her the sad news until the refreshing slumber of another night had strengthened her tired and deeply taxed nerves.

My children, who clung to me so tenderly, and who loved their parent as only children can love, were quietly sleeping in the same room. I alone of that household was wakeful. I alone saw and felt the dense cloud of blackness gathering around us; seemingly ready to burst upon us and destroy our happiness forever. And it did burst, in all its hellish fury; but not before God had assured me that, though I was to walk through the water and the fire, the one should not overflow me, and the other should not harm me.

When day broke I arose from my restless couch and attended to my morning work. During the forenoon I told my wife the dreadful story of the accusation.

She threw her arms around me, and by tender caresses and loving words assured me of her unfaltering trust in my innocence and fidelity.

Had it been otherwise, I know not the result. Had my true, faithful, loving wife thought me guilty of the crime charged, long since would I have been overcome by the almost unbearable burden. As it was, I received new strength and fresh courage. And the consciousness of this unfaltering trust in my faithful wife has cheered and sustained me throughout the terrible months through which I have passed.

As I look back upon the fourth and fifth days of September, 1878, I am both pained and surprised. Up to the 3d of September, the day of the homicide, no one ever thought that I was other than what I seemed.

But now wild rumors filled the air; stories of crime and dark deeds were upon every lip; and the cool, calm judgment of men had run wild. Threats of injury, and shouts of "Hang him!" were freely uttered; and that night, when I lay my weary body down, I knew not but that the next morning would find me a poor, lifeless, shapeless lump of clay.

Before retiring I prayed for that succor which He alone can give. I had just fallen into an uneasy, uncertain slumber, when the noise of an approaching wagon awakened me. Intently I listened. It stopped at the gate. Silently I arose and awaited the result. Very shortly I heard my name whispered. My wife, now thoroughly aroused, begged me not to go. Calming her as best I could I approached the window. Again I heard my name called. "Who's there?" I asked, in as steady a voice as I could command. "A friend," was the answer, and it sent a thrill of joy through my whole being. Yes! a friend was found even in that hour of darkness and despair. Not my neighbor; not my brother church member alone; but that mystic band of men whose brother I am had sent one to counsel and advise with me.

The next morning (Friday) I was arrested by Deputy Sheriff Hull and carried to the probate court office, ten miles from my home. I was immediately put to plea. I pleaded "not guilty," and moved for a continuance in order to secure counsel. This was readily granted, and the court adjourned to Monday, September 9.

Instead of being carried to jail I was put under the care of keepers, two being deemed sufficient for so desperate a criminal. My being put under keepers, instead of behind bars and bolts, was done at the earnest solicitation of the stewards of my church. And here I ought to say that, from the very first, not one of my church and congregation ever believed me guilty of the terrible crime.

All through the long imprisonment that followed my re-arrest I was the constant recipient of tokens of their love and continued confidence. They regarded me as their pastor, and I did work as such throughout the entire time of my incarceration.

THE STANNARD FAMILY.

Religious and kindly interest taken in Mary Stannard.

And now let us carefully seek out and set in order the relations sustained between the Stannards and myself. When I first went to Rockland I was told by the retiring preacher, J. W. Gibbs (who, afterwards, appeared as a witness against me), that a young woman of the neighborhood had just given birth to an illegitimate child.

I inquired into the history of the family, and found that they were of low birth and ill repute.

The family at this time consisted of the father, Charles Sylvester Stannard; a step-daughter, Susan Hawley; and the daughter, Mary Elizabeth Stannard; who was the mother of the new, but unfortunate babe.

On further inquiry I learned that they had but few friends and fewer visitors.

When the mother had recovered sufficiently to attend to household duties, my wife was informed that she felt keenly her position, was penitent and desired to reform. Accordingly she sent for Miss Stannard to call upon her, which she shortly did. After a long, serious conversation, my wife informed me that she had become deeply interested in the young woman, and desired me to encourage her all in my power.

We both felt that we could not cast the first stone; and, hence, set ourselves at work removing the briars and thorns that hedged her pathway.

We encouraged her to attend the regular church services, the Sabbath school, and the stated prayer and class meetings. We also gave her employment when occasion offered.

We always found her faithful in the discharge of her duties, and apparently eager to gain the good will not only of ourselves, but also of all in the community.

Others, encouraged by our example, opened their doors to her; and, before the year of my pastorate in Rockland had closed, Miss Stannard was received into nearly every household in the place.

During this year (1876) and the two following I also employed the father. Day after day have we worked side by side on the farm. Being thus thrown into each other's company, we became more or less free in each other's society; and whenever Mr. Stannard wanted any farm tool or house implement he was welcome to its use. And many are the things, both from the farm and house, which have found their way to his humble home.

During the summer of 1877 my wife taught the district school in the place. As I was busily engaged on the farm, Mary E. Stannard was employed to take care of the children and get the noon-day meal. She would come at 8 o'clock in the morning, and leave at 5 o'clock in the afternoon. During the winter of 1877–8 she was employed to discharge the same duties, with the addition of remaining nights, as I was teaching school at Madison, ten miles from home. As before stated, she would come to the house on Saturday afternoon, and remain till the following Friday evening, when I returned home.

My wife's school closed a fortnight before mine. Leaving Mary in charge of the house, she took the children and visited me in Madison. As a recompense to Mary for this extra work, my wife promised her that, when she received her money, Mr. Hayden would carry her to Middletown, where she could purchase needed supplies. When Mary received her money she spent nearly all of it for groceries at the village store, and it was not until after the huckleberry season had passed that she reminded my wife of her promise.

At my wife's solicitation I carried her to Middletown some four or five weeks previous to the homicide. In January, 1878, an oyster supper was given in the then unoccupied parsonage, for the benefit of the Rockland church. Another was given in the month of March.

At the first oyster supper I would occasionally run over to our house to see that the children were safe.

Finding this method to be unpleasant, at the oyster supper in March we employed Mary Stannard to take care of the children. I returned home about 9 o'clock to put the children to bed, according to my usual custom. I was absent from the oyster supper about ten minutes.

The distance from the parsonage (where the supper was given) to my house is only 228 feet.

My house is situated upon the road leading from Madison to Middletown and Hartford. This road forks just above my house— a branch leading off in an easterly direction, but returning to the main road some three miles above , so that a person going north can take either road according to his fancy.

On the morning of the day of the homicide, September 3, I started for Middletown to purchase some needed articles and to get some carpenter's tools that had been promised me. In Middletown I went to see about the tools ; then went to David Tyler's and purchased a box of fullers' earth for my wife ; also an ounce of arsenic to kill the rats which infested my house and barn. In returning, at Durham I purchased a bag of oats, a gallon of molasses and $1 worth of sugar.

In going to Middletown I took the branch road just above our house, but in returning I came on the main road. This would take me past the Stannard house. When I was opposite the house my children were there, and cried: "Papa, we want to ride home." I stopped the horse and put the children into the carriage. Charles Stannard came out, and I asked him for a drink of water. He said that the water was warm. I tasted of it, but it was unfit to drink, and I threw it away. I then drove towards home. On the road, near a spring of cool, sweet water, I met Mary Stannard, bearing a pail of the precious beverage. I asked for a drink of water, got it, and then drove home.

In the afternoon, as we were out of wood, I went to my wood-lot and threw up some wood in readiness for carting, being absent about one and three-quarter hours. The distance from my house to the wood-lot is 2,905 feet in an easterly direction. From my house to where the body was found is 4,788 feet, in a northwesterly direction, making a distance of nearly a mile and a half between the two points.

It may here be stated that the Sunday after I left home, intending to go to the Vineyard, Mary Stannard went to work in Guilford. She stayed two weeks and then returned home; Mr. Studley, for whom she had been working, bringing her back.

With these details let us return to the court room.

On Monday, at 10 o'clock in the forenoon, the court was opened by the Justice, Henry Beals Wilcox. In the meantime I had secured as counsel L. M. Hubbard, of Wallingford, Conn., and Samuel F. Jones, of Hartford, Conn. The prosecution was conducted by H. Lynde Harrison and James I. Hayes, of New Haven, Conn.; James P. Platt, son of the State's Attorney, of Meriden, Conn.; Judge Langdon, of Guilford, Conn.; and the Grand Juror, Charles Socrates Stannard, of Madison, Conn.

The court was held in the basement of the Congregational church at Madison. This was as inconvenient, uncomfortable and unhandy a place as one can imagine. There was a total lack of ventilation. The walls were low and damp. The sun seldom, if ever, penetrated the gloom ; and the only means of lighting the room was by antiquated lamps. The shadows cast, and the faces, barely discernible in the uncertain light, reminded one of those inquisitorial halls so common in the sixteenth century. Into this dark and damp place I was led by the officers of the law, reminding one of the words of Scripture: "They loved darkness rather than light, because their deeds were evil."

The result of this examination was my release by Justice Wilcox. Subsequently I was arrested on a bench warrant, and held for trial before the Superior Court. Though I earnestly demanded a speedy trial, yet one pretense and another was found to delay it, and for about thirteen months I was kept by the state's representatives in prison ; but I am not disposed to complain, though it is a hard thing to separate an innocent man from his family, and place him in a situation where all means of support are cut off, and where, by the operation of law, which presupposes innocence in every man until guilt is proven, no redress is possible. During all this time my prison life was ameliorated by the kind sympathy of many friends.

REMARKABLE INCIDENTS.

Illustrative of Providential Guidance.

All of the most remarkable incidents of my life seem destined to occur within bird's-eye view of New Haven. When I was fourteen years of age, at a point opposite New Haven, on Long Island Sound, I was one of three actors in a little drama in which a human life was at stake.

We were sailing down the Sound in a small schooner of seventy-five tons burden. The wind, which had been light, had suddenly increased to that degree that it became necessary to shorten sail. This work was nearly completed, when suddenly one of the men was projected into the sea.

I, being at the helm, put it hard to leeward and .brought the vessel head to the wind. The other man being aloft, I ran and let both the jib and foresail sheets loose. At this time I was joined by the other man, and springing to the boat, soon launched it into the sea.

Although but a minute or two had elapsed, we were at a considerable distance from the man. This distance, together with the high sea running, made it highly improbable that the man would ever be saved. But, springing into the boat, I grasped an oar, and, inwardly praying for strength, started on my perilous but merciful mission.

I had nearly reached the man, when, looking around, he was

nowhere to be seen. Continuing to urge the boat forward, I at last espied him as he rose to the surface.

Thinking that I could reach him, I dropped the oar and sprang to the bow of the boat. But a wave at that instant struck the boat and carried it to a distance; at the same time the man again sank beneath the surface. I knew that now was the last chance. I grasped the oar, and, exerting all my strength, speedily recovered my lost ground ; and as he rose to the surface grasped him by the hair of his head.

I had succeeded in my object, had rescued the man from a watery grave, but could do no more. My strength, consequent on the reaction of the excitement and over-exertion, suddenly left me. I was unable to get him into the boat. He had lost all consciousness, but I kept his head above the water. When my strength returned I rolled him into the boat, unconscious as he was.

Up to this time I had no thought of the vessel. Now I looked for it and saw it two or three miles to the leeward.

Here was I, in a gale of wind on the open sea, in an open boat freighted with an unconscious human being ; and to make it still worse, with night approaching. My work was not done. I had still to save both him and myself. Lifting my heart in prayer, I headed for the vessel. By hard work and the help of Him who rides upon the storm I succeeded in reaching the vessel just as the mantle of night fell upon the water. Sailing into New Haven harbor, we remained two or three days, until the man recovered, and then proceeded on our way.

There is another incident of which I will speak, although it occurred many miles from New Haven. It was just after the close of the civil war. We were sailing from New York to Richmond, Va. All went well until we sighted the capes of Chesapeake, when the wind suddenly changed and came in dead ahead. From a stiff breeze it soon became a living gale. At first we shortened sail, but finally were forced to scud before it under bare poles. Night came on, and the darkness was intense. The wind increased, until it fairly shrieked as it passed through the rigging. The waves ran mountain high, and seemed like huge devouring monsters hastening to their prey. All through this long, dark and fearful night we were driven like chaff before the wind. The vessel, now borne upon the crest of the waves and anon sinking into the trough of the sea, labored, and creaked, and groaned, until it seemed as if every moment would be her last. But with her freight of precious souls she safely drove before the gale.

Towards morning the wind began to abate. Just at the break of day a thick, appalling cloud of darkness bore down upon us. Swiftly it came, but spent its force before it reached us. It was followed by another—not of wind, but of rain. The rain fell in torrents, and when the cloud passed to seaward not a breath of air remained.

For a short time we kept stern to the waves, but finally the vessel bore round into the trough of the sea. Now the vessel began to roll. At every roll her bulwarks were buried beneath the waves, and the water surged across the deck. It seemed as if the masts would snap asunder, and, to make bad matters worse, the vessel began to leak. All hands were called to the pumps ; but, owing to the heavy rolling of the vessel, little or no progress could be made. It was a terrible moment with us. Hearts, which never before had prayed, were now uplifted in fervent supplication. Strong men, who had laughed defiance at many a gale, trembled as they looked upon the water.

There was one hope left. Our boat had not been stove. But could it live in such a sea? We were resolved to try, for we knew that if we remained we should perish. We secured the necessary charts and provisions, and succeeded in safely launching the boat. But before the order, "Man the boat," came, hope feebly revived in our breasts. The waves had somewhat abated, while far out over the water could be seen a cloud rising out of the sea.

We again manned the pumps, and shortly a faint zephyr fell upon us. This was followed by another and still another, until, loosening the sails, they caught the breeze, and the noble vessel, wearing round, sped safely on her way.

These experiences may have no special interest to the public now ; but as I write in my close quarters in jail they have a satisfying influence upon my own thoughts, giving renewed assurance of the protecting power of Almighty God in times of great danger and distress ; and, as I close this hurriedly written narrative, I am moved to give thanks to Him who has so far given me strength in every trial and afforded succor in every dark and perilous way through which I have passed in my life's pilgrimage—and upon His strong arm I now lean with the fullest measure of confidence in His grace and peace.

HERBERT H. HAYDEN.

New Haven Jail, December, 1879.

WHERE MARY E. STANNARD'S BODY WAS FOUND.

[The stake represents where her head was lying, the body inclining on the ground as shown by the boards. The pail shows where the one she took with her to get blackberries was discovered when she was found dead.]

MR. HAYDEN IN THE TRIAL.

The examination of Mr. Hayden occupied the greater part of four days. When his name was first called the court-room was all attention, and all eyes were directed to the coming witness, who with self-possession took the stand. Mr. Watrous desired Mr. Jones to inquire.

Mr. Jones—Mr. Hayden, what's your age?

Answer—Twenty-nine.

Mr. Jones—Mr. Hayden, I want to ask you a general question. (Deep stillness.) First, have you any knowledge of the time, place, manner or person, and by whom, if any, and when or where Mary Stannard came to her death?

The answer was awaited with profound stillness.

The prisoner responded clearly and distinctly—None whatever.

Mr. Jones—Mr. Hayden, what is your occupation?

Mr. Hayden—I was a preacher in charge of the church at South Madison. The place where I lived in Rockland was one I rented; had lived there since April, 1877; came to Rockland in April, 1876; had lived a year in another house—the parsonage. That first year in Rockland I was the preacher in charge of the church there—placed in charge by the presiding elder, William T. Hill. Yes, sir; the present presiding elder. The next place I preached at was South Madison.

Mr. Watrous—Not quite so fast, Mr. Jones, please.

Witness—I was preaching constantly while living in Rockland;

from April, 1877, till the 12th of August, 1877, there was an intermission ; otherwise I worked at my trade—carpentering—and also teaching school ; taught school at South Madison from October, 1877, till March, 1878. During that time my wife was teaching in Rockland district, the school commencing, I think, a week later than mine, and ending a fortnight before mine ; I am not quite certain on that point.

Mr. Watrous to Mr. Jones—Wait a moment for me to write.

Witness—That is correct, I think. Her winter term did not begin until after mine. No ; I don't recollect, Mr. Jones, how many terms my wife taught.

Mr. Jones—Well, that's not important.

Witness—I came to Rockland from West Rocky Hill. Lived in West Rocky Hill one year or thereabouts. As to my occupation, I was preacher in charge of the church—Methodist. Prior to that I lived at Middletown. Lived there from July 3, 1873, to April, 1875, and was there to complete my education. Was in college in Middletown. The last year while there I preached every Sabbath at West Rocky Hill church, the church where I was stationed the next year. In vacations I worked at my trade. The occasion of my leaving Middletown was on account of my health. It was a head trouble.

I was in the sophomore class when I left. I came to Middletown from East Greenwich Conference Seminary, where I had been four years and graduated. I was married August 8, 1871. During this time my wife was teaching school. She did not teach in Greenwich, but in a town outside. She taught at Middletown.

Mr. Jones—Have you ever been upon a witness stand in your life before the Madison trial?

Witness—No, sir.

Mr. Waller asked the object of this.

Mr. Jones—I see no reason for an objection. It is simply to show that he is not a trained witness.

Witness—On the Sunday before the homicide was in South Madison preaching. Left home at 9 o'clock Sabbath morning. Yes ; I had had a room in South Madison. When teaching in the town the winter previous I had a room at the house of Norman Scranton. I preached at South Madison that day once, and attended Sabbath school and evening prayer-meeting. In the previous year I preached twice there Sundays. Left home in my own team. No one was with me. Left to return home at 1 o'clock Monday afternoon. It was my usual custom so to do, only I would leave a little earlier in the day. During haying season I came home Sunday night, and during my wife's confinement I came home then. I stayed till 1 on that Monday, as I had to get my horse shod. I wished to see my stewards, and had to go to Hammonassett to see about a school for myself to teach for the coming winter. That is a school district of Madison. No; my salary did not permit me to live without extra work. I saw three—yes, four of my stewards that day. They were Norman Scranton, William Minor, Thomas Pendelow and ——— Dudley—his first name don't come to me now —Lancelot, it was. One of them lived north, William Minor lived a mile or more away, and Thomas Pendelow two miles, and Lancelot Dudley half a mile further off. These are rough estimates.

Mr. Jones—Did you go to the house of each?

Witness—I did. I took dinner that day at Norman Scranton's. Got my horse shod in the morning between 8 and 9. Started for home about 1. Brought along a few apples, a half peck of oysters in the shell, about a peck of pears and a watermelon. Mrs. N. Scranton gave me the apples; Thomas Pendelow gave me the oysters, pears and the watermelon. I do not remember particularly with regard to the day. It was warm and sultry, I think. Arrived home at about 3 p. m. No one was with me. No one was in the house that I remember except my wife and children—yes, two children and the baby. After getting home I took care of my horse. I carried the articles which had been given me into the house, put the oysters down cellar, the rest of the things elsewhere. I then sat down in the dining-room, read a paper and smoked.

Mr. Jones—That's a fault you have?

Witness—A good fault, I think.

Witness—I sat at the dining-room window. Yes, sir; it does look over to the wood lot. As I sat reading and smoking, it being about 4 o'clock, Mary Stannard came into the room and said that her father wished the rake.

Mr. Watrous—Wait a moment! Mr. Hayden, where was your wife then?

Witness—She was sitting at the north dining-room window holding the baby.

Mr. Jones—Is that the window over which there has been so much controversy?

Witness—It is.

Mr. Jones—State in your own way what transpired.

Witness—When Mary said she wanted the rake, I nodded my head, finished the paragraph I was reading, and rose to go to the barn. Mary had taken the baby in her arms from my wife. The dining-room windows were open and the door was open. I went to the barn and got a rake, and returned to the house. As I—

Mr. Jones—Now go slowly. It may be unpleasant to you, but we want to write it all.

Witness—I saw Mary coming from the dining-room door. She stepped off the piazza, and asked me for the rake and how long she could keep it. I told her my work was done, and I was in no hurry for it.

Mr. Jones—Where was your wife and where was Mary when she asked how long she could keep it?

Witness—Mary was standing near me on the ground, just off the piazza, on the path by the porch ; by the porch I mean the ell.

Mr. Jones—There was nothing more said·by you to Mary or by Mary to you?

Witness—No, sir.

Mr. Jones—Did Mary go to your barn that day?

Witness—She did not at that time.

Mr. Jones—Wait a moment. What did you do then, Mr. Hayden?

Witness—I went to my house and resumed my reading. Mary went toward the gate.

Mr. Jones—Did you notice her after that?

Witness—I did not.

Mr. Jones—Did you have any conversation with Mary except as stated, and except in the presence of your wife?

Witness—I did not.

Mr. Jones—That all may see what you have said, it being a matter about which all should be clear, will you point out where you were when you delivered the rake to the girl? [Taking to Mr. Hayden a photograph. Witness pointed and stated.]

Mr. Jones—Was Mary at that visit any nearer your barn than the spot you have indicated?

Witness—Not when I saw her, and I have no reason to suppose she was any nearer

Mr. Jones—Do you remember how you went into the barn—through the door or the aperture?

Witness—Through the large door.

Mr. Watrous—The large door through which you drove a load of hay?

Witness—Yes, sir.

Mr. Jones—After that you resumed reading and smoking?

Witness—I did.

Mr. Jones—What else occurred that afternoon?

Witness—About half-past 4 George Davis came in to see if I could work for him. I don't know whether I had got through smoking then or not. Mr. Davis lives away a good three miles in the town of Killingworth. He wished me to come and work with him in his lot.

Mr. Jones—Did you arrange with him?

Witness—I did. I was to go Wednesday morning. I told him in the first place I did not see how I could come as I had not got in all my potatoes. He said he should have a number of days' work for me. I said I would like to have him average so that I could work for him and do my own work too. He was at the house only a few moments.

Mr. Jones—What else occurred that Monday afternoon of any importance?

Witness—I don't know of anything.

Mr. Jones—Did you see Mary Stannard that day or her father that day?

Witness—I did not.

Mr. Jones—Nothing else occurred?

Witness—Not that I recollect now.

Mr. Jones—Mr. Hayden, were you alone with Mary Stannard that day?

Witness—I was not.

Mr. Jones—Or have any conversation with her as stated?

Witness—There was none.

Mr. Jones—Had you at that time, Mr. Hayden, any knowledge that Mary Stannard was in fact, or pretended to be, in a peculiar position?

Witness—I had no knowledge of it.

Mr. Jones—Did the thought enter your mind?

Witness—It did not.

Mr. Jones—Did you have any conversation, that day or the day prior to that, or on any day, on that subject, of any kind?

Witness—I did not.

Mr. Jones—Was there any reason why you should think there was?

Witness—No reason under the sun.

Mr. Jones—Mr. Hayden, were you ever criminally intimate with that girl? [Deep silence in the court-room.]

Witness—I never was. Never!

Mr. Jones—Breaking the chain a moment, what was the condition of your house so far as to its being infested with vermin?

Witness—It was infested with vermin.

Mr. Jones—With what?

Witness—Rats. Yes, sir; I had a conversation on the subject with Thomas Pendelow. It was the Sunday before that, August 11th, that Mary Stannard went to Mrs. Studley's to live. I spoke with Mr. Pendelow at South Madison. He told me that he by all means would buy arsenic. I told him that my wife was opposed to it, strongly opposed to my having poison of any kind in the house. I remember when we first moved to Rockland we found in the parsonage a bottle labeled "Poison." She said that she would not have it in the house, and made me take it out and destroy it. I had talked with her about buying arsenic. She was strongly opposed to it. That was before I had talked with Pendelow. I don't remember of talking with any one else about buying it. No; I did not fully make up my mind to buy after that conversation with Mr. Pendelow.

Mr. Jones—Mr. Hayden, when was it that you settled, and what was the occasion, to buy arsenic?

Witness—It was during the last week in August, when I found that the whortleberries we had preserved had been destroyed. They had been put in a jar covered with paper, either tied or sealed down, and the rats had gnawed through the paper and intermingled with the berries. I do not recollect whether it was my wife or Mrs. Davis who discovered it. I think it was my wife. My wife at that time was not able to go down cellar. If my wife called my attention to it, they had been brought up stairs. I then resolved to get arsenic.

Mr. Jones—Were you going to tell your wife about it?

Witness—I was not.

Mr. Jones—You say you fully determined. Did you say anything to anybody of your intention?

Witness—I did; I think, with Mrs. Davis present, I said: "I shall certainly doctor the rats." I did not tell my wife of my intention.

Mr. Jones—What was your wife's condition then?

Witness—She was in feeble health and very nervous. She mentioned ratsbane as the thing she would have no objection to my getting.

Mr. Jones—Did you know at that time that arsenic and ratsbane were identical?

Witness—I did not until Professor Johnson so said. I had before that had Paris green, and always kept it in the barn.

Mr. Jones—That contains arsenic, does it not?

Witness—I could not tell you.

Mr. Jones—It's pretty much all arsenic. Now we will come down to Tuesday. Did you leave home Tuesday?

Witness—I did, shortly after 6 a. m. I went away to get feed for my horse—oats. It was the occasion of my going away. I did not get them at South Madison Monday, as I had no account at South Madison. I had store accounts at Durham, at Leach's and Davis's.

Mr. Jones—You had a little homeopathic account at Rockland, at a little store there?

Witness—I did not go there, as sometimes they had oats and sometimes not. I did see some one before I went away. I saw Charles Stannard. I did hear Mr. Stannard testify.

Mr. Jones—Where was he—the precise place now—when you saw him?

Witness—I was going from the house to the wood-pile. He wished me to draw his hay that afternoon. I had drawn it for him the year previous. It was not at all unusual for him to make such requests or to borrow little things.

Mr. Jones—What articles did he borrow?

Witness—I can't remember. He felt perfectly free to come.

[Mr. Hayden during recess returned to his seat. With him were, in this momentous period of the trial, his wife, father and mother, brother and wife's brother, who all talked with him, and gave him smiles and cheer ; and two or three other family friends. Mr. Hayden told his story to the court in a straightforward way, with every indication of frankness, and made a good impression.]

Mr. Jones—Mr. Stannard wished you to haul some hay ; what occurred ?

Witness—I told him that in the morning I had got to go away, and in the afternoon to draw wood. I am not positive whether I said draw or get. I don't think that I told him definitely where I was going, but simply going away. I went to get oats, molasses, fullers' earth for the house, some tools for myself, some arsenic for the rats.

Mr. Jones—Had you, when you left the house, made up your mind to go to Middletown ? A.—I had not.

Mr. Jones—What did you want the fullers' earth for ?

Witness—For use. Well, persons, whether old or young, chafe. Yes ; I have some at present in my cell. I went one way to Middletown, and came back the other. It was more according to habit that I did so, and the right hand road was the easier to go and the other the easier to return. Besides, it was a pleasanter way on a hot day.

Mr. Jones—Will you point out the road ?

Witness (pointing on the map)—It was when in Durham that I decided to go to Middletown. When I got to Durham I found that it was but little after 7 o'clock, that my horse was in good condition, it was still cool, and I wished to see about some tools. I did not suppose that they kept fullers' earth at Durham. Do not remember seeing any one on the way. I remember that Fillmore Scranton and Wilbur Stevens testified to meeting me between Durham Center and my home.

Mr. Jones—Did you meet them ?

Witness—I did not. At 8 o'clock I was in Middletown. The first place I went to was Lafayette Burton's. I went into the house ; saw Mrs. Burton ; her husband was out. I cannot positively state that she said where he was, but I think she said at the Industrial School. The time next before that I stopped at the house was August 13. Next prior to that I had been there in May, I think and next before that in March. I made arrangements with Burton in the fall of 1877, contracting with him for a lumber wagon. I was to pay him money for the iron, and produce for the wood-work. I did not know how much it was to cost me, but it was somewhere in the neighborhood of $45. I had had previous acquaintance with him. We talked it over, and thought it would cost about $45. The produce was things I raised on the farm, turnips, potatoes, or anything that I raised that I had. That was arranged in the fall of 1877. The vegetables were to be delivered at any time that he wished. Had known Burton as far back as 1873. Had lived in the house with him at one time. Was a man in whom I had confidence. The arrangement was broken up the 1st of March, 1878. I had delivered him at that time $9 or $10 worth of vegetables. My wife bought me a wagon with her school money, and then I went to Middletown and told Burton that I needed not the wagon.

Mr. Jones—Your good wife bought the wagon with the avails of her teaching?

Witness—Yes. Mr. Burton and I agreed as to tools in place of the wagon. He agreed (it was in February) to pay me for what he had received in tools. I told him I should need some bits, a plow, some machinist's tools, a drill, some callipers and a square. Mr. Burton at that time worked for the Star Tool Company.

Mr. Jones—That concern was then in full life?

Witness—Well, I can't say that.

Mr. Jones—It had been running down for some time?

Witness—Yes, sir; he went to work then for the Industrial School. The tools were to be delivered at his house. Every time I went I was told that I should surely have the tools the next time. I was quite anxious for the bit to drill iron with. I did not then, nor do I now know, where the Industrial School is. I knew the general direction. No; one does not pass in sight of the school in going. I lived last on Cross street. High is the street running by the college. You could not see the building from Cross street from where I lived. By walking up a distance I could see the buildings. They appeared to be two miles away.

Mr. Jones—That is the institution where naughty girls are sent?

Witness—So they say. Yes; if asked independent of what I have heard in court, I should say it was three miles away. I drove by the building once after I had moved to Rockland. It was either with Fillmore Scranton or Walter Green. I was surprised at hearing Mr. Burton say he could walk there in fifteen minutes. I didn't turn off that 3d of September and drive up there first, because, when the tools were done, they were to be at the house, and, second, because I did not know where the buildings were. I do not see now, from what Mr. Harrison has said, the exact location. Burton's house, in reference to Tyler's drug store, is a mile north.

Mr. Jones—Oh! then I am all in a fog about that point.

Witness—I was at Mr. Burton's that day but a few moments. I don't think I ever saw the Industrial School when on my way to Middletown. I staid at Burton's three or four minutes. I then went to Tyler's drug store. I hitched my horse in the shade. I went there direct from last place. George Tyler was there. I had been there before. I couldn't enumerate the number of times I had been in that drug store. I had known Mr. Tyler since 1873. I bought all my Paris green there, fullers' earth and all my articles in the apothecary's line. No one else was there but George. I asked George Tyler if he had fullers' earth there. He went to the back part of the store to get it. I don't know further than that he went into the back part. Whether he went down cellar I can't tell. When he returned he brought fullers' earth. He had a coarse, unground, unpulverized, I should say, article. I told him I wanted better. He said: "We've another kind," and went and got some. I think I was looking over some gift almanacs while he was away.

Mr. Jones (obtaining a pad of blotting paper) asked Mr. Hayden to draw a sketch of that store. Mr. Hayden employed himself thus for a minute or two.

Witness—The store faces the highway from Main street. A counter and show-case upon it is on the right. I stood at the show-case next the shed while George was gone. [The lawyers gathered around witness.] The gift almanacs were here (pointing to the diagram). After I told him that I desired a better article, he says: "We have it." After he had carried the first batch back, he went to the show-case and showed me an article put up in boxes. I should think of that depth (designating).

Mr. Watrous—About three inches?

Witness—Yes, sir. I approved of it. At this point David came to the store. As I said it he (George) moved back to the scales. The cigar case is there and the soda case there (pointing). I then

THE SPRING.

[Where Mary E. Stannard went after water the day Mr. Hayden returned from Middletown, on the morning of the murder.]

told Mr. David Tyler that I wanted an ounce of arsenic for rats. He put it up. George was then doing up fullers' earth. I sat down in a chair opposite No. 2 counter, about opposite the scales and nearest the road. I don't remember as I did anything more than look at a gift almanac. I do not know where David got the arsenic. I do not know whether it was from a bottle, a package, or an open box. I did not watch. I told him I wanted an ounce of arsenic, and he proceeded to get it. David did it up. The whole cost thirty-five cents—the fullers' earth twenty-five cents, the arsenic ten. The arsenic was marked " Poison " by David. When I spoke about arsenic two ladies came into the store, and George went to wait upon them. I do not know who they were. They were strangers. I had a Peruvian dollar in my pocket. I asked him how much it was worth. He said eighty-five cents; that he had one in his till, and he wished he could get rid of it. I handed him a dollar bill, and he took out the thirty-five cents. Nothing else happened in the store of any importance. I was in the store about ten minutes. When I went into the store I made inquiry for David Tyler. George said he had just stepped out to the post office for the mail. As I stepped away from the store I saw Dr. Bailey. He was our family physician. He had never been to Rockland; but we had been to Middletown to consult him.

Mr. Jones—Did not your wife say he called to see your little boy? A.—Did she? I do not recollect it.

Mr. Jones—Do you know Walter Green, of Rockland?

Witness—Yes, sir.

Mr. Jones—Do you remember that he was attended by Dr. Bailey? It may refresh your recollection.

Witness—Oh, yes: I remember that, as I fetched the doctor for him; but I can't recollect that the doctor visited us. Yes: it was I stopped Dr. Bailey.

Mr. Jones—Whom did you meet when driving home?

Witness—I met in the first place Duell Stevens in Middletown. He knew me. I knew him. He was unloading charcoal at the next house north of Burton's. Stevens lived in Rockland, the next house south of me. Yes, in short, was a neighbor of mine.

Mr. Jones—You didn't try to keep out of sight of him?

Witness—I did not. When driving out of Middletown I met again Duell Stevens, and soon after met Sereno Scranton.

Mr. Jones—Do you mean Sereno of Madison?

Witness—Oh! I don't mean this one here, but S. S. Scranton. Lives in Durham. I had met him at the Vineyard. He gave me reports of father's and mother's health. [A tear stood in the eye of witness' father.] I can't say that I met any one else on my way until I got to Durham. I may have passed several teams.

Mr. Jones—Didn't try to hide yourself? No occasion for that?

Witness—No, sir.

Mr. Jones—How far is it from your house to New Haven?

Witness—Twenty miles.

Mr. Jones—Prior to the time you were brought here and locked up in this jail, did you know any New Haven druggists?

Witness—I did not, nor do I now, except one. On my way back from Durham I bought at Durham a bushel of oats and a gallon of molasses.

Mr. Jones—Did you get rid of that Peruvian dollar?

Witness (smiling a little)—No, I got trusted. The post office was in the store of Leach, where I bought the oats, etc. I got a letter there for my wife and one for Silas Y. Ives.

Mr. Jones—Did you have or had you any reason for stopping at any place after leaving Durham?

Witness—None whatever. It was a very warm and sultry day. Yes ; my horse panted. I made my first stop in the road in front of Charles Stannard's because my little girl said: "Papa, I want to ride home." No; I had not up to that time any knowledge that my children were at Stannard's. My little girl was standing in front. I was some twenty or thirty feet north of a spot in the road opposite their gate.

Mr. Jones—Did you stop there?

Witness—I did. I partially pulled my horse out of the road when I heard my little girl. The point was nearly opposite the gate. [Witness pointed it out for Mr. Jones in a little pencil sketch.] The next person I saw was Charlie Stannard. He came around to the corner of the house, came out the gate, and as I stopped my team he was behind me. The carriage was, oh, I should think, all of eight feet away. I spoke to him and he to me. I do not remember what was said then. Before I had got out of my wagon my little girl was joined by my little boy. I jumped out of the wagon and put in Lenny and Emma, and when I turned round to speak to Mr. Stannard again, Ben Stevens and Mary Stannard were standing inside the fence, leaning upon it.

Mr. Jones—Now, Mr. Hayden, without my asking any question of you, I wish you would give all the details of what was said and done there.

Witness—I'll give it to you as I remember. Mr. Stevens spoke and said it was a warm day, and asked if I had driven far. I said yes, from Middletown. Then I turned to Mr. Stannard and asked him for a drink of water. I had been smoking, and the weather was very dry. He said yes, and I gave the reins to Emma, who was in the wagon, and followed Stannard into the house. We went into the front door and into the hall.

Mr. Waller—I did not get that. Witness carefully repeated it.

Witness—We passed from there to the front room, from there to the kitchen, to the pantry. Mr. Stannard took a glass and lifted me some water from a pail. I tasted it, told him it was warm, and threw the water out of the window and handed back the glass. We then followed the same route back to the door. Probably I should have stated that Susan Hawley was in the kitchen, and I said to her: "Good morning." Also said good morning to Mary Stannard. As I went out Stevens and Mary still stood in the same place where I left them.

Mr. Waller—Where? Mr. Jones—Hanging on to the fence.

Witness—I then got into the wagon, and then—I cannot tell how the conversation opened, but Mr. Stevens and I got talking about some lumber at Mr. Hills's.

Mr. Jones—You may state the conversation.

Witness—August 9 James Hill had a barn blown down. The conversation was about a Southern pine floor which Stevens said he had been trying to purchase for Lemuel Scranton. He said he hadn't made much headway in the purchase because Fillmore Scranton and Nehemiah Burr were outbidding him. He stated that he thought it was worth $16, but Hill wanted $20, and Mr. Lemuel Scranton did not want him to give over $17. While we were engaged in this conversation Mary had left us; shortly re-appeared with a pail, and told her father she was going to the spring for a pail of water.

Mr. Jones—You may state right here if that's the only place for their getting water? A.—It is.

Mr. Jones—On what subject did you have conversation with Benjamin Stevens at Stannard's house?

Witness—I talked about the weather and other common-place subjects.

Mr. Jones—What time was this?

Witness—It was shortly after 11 o'clock.

Mr. Jones—Was Mary anywhere in sight? A.—No, sir.

Mr. Jones—If you saw Mary anywhere about that time, you may state.

Witness—As I was on my way home in the carriage, I met Mary coming with a pail of water.

Mr. Jones—How far should you think it was from Stannard's house down to the spring?

Witness—I should think about forty rods.

Mr. Jones—If you were in your carriage looking southerly, how soon would a person pass out of view after leaving Stannard's house going to the spring?

Witness—I should think about half the distance.

Mr. Jones—Mr. Hayden, before continuing your story, I desire to take you back to the barn. You said when you entered the barn to get the rake you entered by the large door. Why did you do this?

Witness—The reason was because the barn was not accessible at that time by the small door, one of the hinges being broken off. I had also commenced to board up that spot. At this time I had no stalls in the barn, and my horse was in one corner. At that time I fed my horse from a firkin, and hitched him to a post that was within four or five feet of the corner of the barn. I boarded up the open space in the northeast corner so that the horse could not get his feet over.

Mr. Jones—Where did you usually enter the barn?

Witness—By the big door.

Mr. Jones—Now let me take you back to the spring. You may state where you met Mary.

Witness—When I started for home from Stannard's, I met Mary north of the spring on the road. She had come out of the pasture lot and stepped into the road before I saw her. I stopped my horse and asked Mary for a drink of water. My little girl was sitting in the carriage, on the left side, nearest the spring. I got out of the carriage because it was inconvenient for her to pass the water to me.

Mr. Jones—What conversation did you have with Mary at that time?

Witness—She gave me a drink of water and I thanked her. There was no other conversation between us.

Mr. Jones—Did you, at the spring or in any other place, have any other conversation with Mary than what you have stated?

Witness—I did not.

Mr. Jones—By signs or otherwise? A.—I did not.

Mr. Jones—Where did you go then? I mean after you left Mary? A.—I went home.

Mr. Jones—Had you ever made any arrangements previous to this time to meet Mary anywhere?

Witness—No, sir. I had not.

Mr. Jones—Had you ever been at the "Big Rock," so called, or did you know where it was?

Witness—I did not. In the winter of 1876 and 1877 I went up into the woods pointing in the direction of the "Big Rock" with Mr. Scranton, who then lived in the Luzerne Stevens house, to see about some wood, and came out somewhere on to this old road. That is the only time that I recollect of ever being in that vicinity.

Mr. Jones—Do you recollect of ever going blackberrying with Luzerne Stevens?

Witness—I have been whortleberrying with him, but not in this vicinity. I went with him up into the woods back of the old parsonage.

Mr. Jones—You say you got home between 11 and 12 o'clock. Now state in detail just what you did?

Witness—I unhitched the horse, put him in the barn and rubbed him down. Went into the house and took off my false bosom and collar, put on my old pants, and then went to my carriage, took out the oats, carried them into the house and placed them in the store-room. Then I carried the sugar and molasses into the house and placed these articles in the buttery. Then I took down an empty tin spice box and went to the barn. I then took the arsenic, poured it into the box and placed it away.

Mr. Jones—Why did you put the arsenic in the box?

Witness—For convenience and safety.

Mr. Jones—Where did you put the arsenic?

Witness—I put it in the barn, in the south-east corner, under or over the hay and on the stringer.

Mr. Jones—How old was your babe at this time?

Witness—Three or four weeks old.

Mr. Jones—Did you tell your wife at this time that you had purchased the arsenic?

Witness—I did not, because I knew she was opposed to it, and she being in feeble health I did not want to worry her.

Mr. Jones—What kind of a shirt did you have on that day?

Witness—A checked shirt.

Mr. Jones—By the way, what did you do after you went into the house from the barn?

Witness—I took some shell oysters that I had brought home and opened them, out under the fir tree. I then took the oysters to my wife and she cooked them. I held the baby. After the oysters were cooked I ate my dinner. Then I took the baby again and she made toast and ate her dinner. After she got through I cleaned the table, swept the kitchen and brushed off the stove. I don't think the dishes were washed right after dinner.

Mr. Jones—Where was the knife when you brought the oysters in?

Witness—It was in my hand open. My wife said she wanted it to peel pears with, and I gave it to her. The oysters were in a white two-quart earthen dish.

Mr. Jones—Where was she when you handed Mrs. Hayden the oysters?

Witness—She was in the kitchen, but at what point I cannot say.

Mr. Jones—For what had that knife been used, Mr. Hayden?

Witness—I had used it for cutting turnips, beefsteak, chicken and various other purposes. The knife was in the house more than half the time.

Mr. Jones—When did you first see that knife after the homicide?

Witness—On Wednesday afternoon. From the time I gave this knife to my wife on Tuesday I did not have it in my possession until the time I have named. I then found it on the kitchen shelf.

Mr. Jones—How long had you owned that knife?

Witness—I think I bought it in January, 1878, when I first went to teaching at South Madison. I know nothing about the so-called found knife. I never saw it until it was produced in court. The large "boy" knife I bought in New Haven while Moody and Sankey were there. I told my little boy, if he would be good and stay at home, I would get him a knife, and I did so.

Mr. Jones—Now we will go back to the house. What did you do after you ate dinner on that Tuesday?

Witness—I went to the barn and fed my horse, then returned to the house and did the chamber work. I then sat down with my wife and read over an inventory of an estate in which my wife had an interest. It was a detailed statement of the expenses of the administrator on the estate of my wife's mother.

Mr. Jones—How long were you and your wife examining that account?

Witness—Oh, I should think about twenty minutes. We looked it over carefully, and I signed it. The administrator was Samuel Shaw, my wife's brother.

Mr. Jones—What did you do after this?

Witness—I took a chair, turned it down on the floor, placed a pillow upon it, and then laid down and commenced playing with my children. While playing with them I told my wife I must go over to the swamp and throw up some wood preparatory to carting. We were out of wood at this time. This was not the first time I had been over there and thrown up wood. I always did so before carting it. I had thrown up wood at the same place for Gilbert Stone. I think this was in the latter part of 1877 or first of 1878. [Witness here pointed out on the map where he threw up the wood for Mr. Stone.] I owned the lot where I got my wood. I bought the wood on it in the winter of 1877 and 1878. When the wood lot was bought, the right of way was reserved by way of the Burr barn and also by way of Silas Y. Ives's barn. The deed of the land called for five or six acres, more or less.

Mr. Jones—Could a man drive over this lot at all times with a pair of cattle?

Witness—No, sir; I don't think he could, on account of the swampy nature of the ground.

Mr. Jones—Now we will go back to the time when you started for the wood lot. What time was it when you started?

Witness—It was after two o'clock, but I don't think it was half-past two. I went out of the kitchen door facing the street. My children accompanied me to the fork of the road, and then I sent them back. In the neighborhood of Stevens's barn I looked back and saw my wife sitting at the window, and threw her a kiss.

Mr. Jones—Was this an unusual occurrence for you?

Witness—No, sir; it was not.

Mr. Jones—Now tell us just what route you took to the wood lot.

Witness—I went up to the Burr barn, then across the open space by my turnip patch, then on to Mr. Burr's lot, then on to Gilbert Stone's lot, till I struck the road; then down to the lot.

Mr. Jones—What way had you generally taken to the wood lot?

Witness—I think I may say truthfully that I almost always went by the way of the Burr barn.

Mr. Jones—What clothing did you have on?

[Witness picked up the clothing he had on, which had been brought in by the sheriff, and selected out the pants, shirt and hat that he wore on that day.]

Mr. Jones—Do you recollect how many piles of wood you threw up on that day?

Witness—I think there were six or seven piles.

Mr. Jones—You may state in what condition you found the wood.

Witness—I found much of it overgrown by vines and brush, and many of the sticks were sunk into the ground. I found it difficult to lift some of the sticks. I thought I threw up about four such loads as my horse could draw. The day was warm and I took it easy. Should think I was there over an hour. As I picked up the wood I would throw some of it toward the road. Other sticks I would take up and carry. Some of the wood was eight or ten inches in diameter, and about five feet in length. The wood was made up of oak, birch and maple.

Mr. Jones—If that wood had been lying free, and easy to pick up and handle, how much sooner could you have moved it?

Witness—Under those circumstances I think I could have done it in half the time.

Mr. Jones—Under the circumstances in which you found the wood, what is the quickest possible time that you could have thrown it up if there had been a hundred thousand dollars at stake?

MR. HAYDEN'S ROCKLAND RESIDENCE IN SUMMER

Witness--I should try to have done it in half an hour.

Mr. Jones—Now indicate on the map the route that you took on your way home.

Witness pointed out on the map the route he took.

Mr. Jones—What time did you get home?

Witness—I think about 4 o'clock.

Mr. Jones—Did you see any of your family before you got home?

Witness—I did. When I got to my potato patch I saw my little girl Emma. I was then near my house. [Witness pointed out on one of the photographs where he was when he saw his little girl.] I called to her to bring me a basket. My wife, I think, was sitting near the east sitting-room window. She replied that there were chips in the basket. I went into the house and poured the chips into the wood-box. I then went into the potato lot and picked up about a peck of potatoes that I had dug the night before. Emma helped me pick them up.

Mr. Jones—How came you to dig the potatoes?

Witness—Luzerne Stevens asked me the afternoon before how my potatoes were turning out, and I told him to come and see. We went to the potato lot, and I pulled up two or three hills. These were the same that I picked up on the following day.

Mr. Jones—Where did you carry the potatoes, if you can remember all these little details?

Witness—Into the cellar. I then asked my little girl if she had picked up the chips, and after that I went up stairs and took off my working shirt and put on a white one.

Mr. Jones—Was this always your custom?

Witness—It was. Made a change when through the heavy farm work. Yes; it was raining. [This was the time Mr. Stannard said he became alarmed about Mary, and went to look for her.] I did several chores and made fire for supper. I don't recollect what we had. Think it was a light supper. No one was visiting with us. Saw Jennie Stevens. I was told there was a person down-stairs when I was changing my shirt. When I came back he was gone. He was Henry Davis, a peddler. Took a letter for us. I played with the children just before and after supper. I was running the chair down as stated. After I had done my chores I went into my study and began a postal card to Jason Dudley, of Hammonassett, in reference to a school about which I had seen him the day before. Mr. Dudley pressed me to take the school. I told him I could not consent to take it until I had consulted with my wife and family. While I was writing the letter Burton Mills came up to a point of the road about there (pointing on map).

Mr. Jones—Well, Mr. Hayden, that was where you were notified of the homicide. Before going into that I want to ask you about a few other matters. You have already said you had made an arrangement to go to work for Mr. George Davis on Wednesday morning. Why didn't you draw a load of wood home?

Witness—I never went to the wood lot until I had prepared wood for loading. It was my intention to draw a load of wood from there Tuesday night, when it was cool. But I had driven my horse considerably for the three days previously, and the day before had driven him twenty-five miles. I preferred he should stand in the cool of the stable than to have him stand in the swamp of the wood lot, annoyed by flies and mosquitoes. The rain hindered me from drawing the load that afternoon.

Mr. Jones—Now you may go on about being notified about the homicide.

Witness—While sitting by the window writing, Burton Mills came up and said to me : "Mary Stannard has been found with her throat cut, upon the Brag lot." I do not know the reason of its being called Brag lot. I had heard of the term. I went out into the kitchen and got my hat, and went out into the road, and Luzerne Stevens was there. I asked Mrs. Stevens if Jennie could stay with my wife. She said yes, and Burton Stevens, Luzerne and myself started for the spot. Luzerne led. [Pointed out on the map as he proceeded.] I started from here, went here. We met no one, I think, on the way. Found there Mr. Mills, his son Freddie, Nehemiah Burr, Andrew Hazen—his name has been called here Hazlett—Fillmore Scranton, Charles Stannard, the father, and a stranger whom I knew not. Have heard since that his name was Mark Collins. After a while Sylvester Scranton and another Rockland man came. After we started Charles Stannard, Andrew Hazen and myself came down the road to about there [pointing].

Mr. Waller—The same Hazen?

Witness—Yes, sir. We came down the road to a coal-pit hut, which lay about here. We took two old blankets that were in the hut, a wide board and two or three short sticks, and returned to the body.

Mr. Jones—Now, Mr. Hayden, to go back a moment. Was anything said, and, if so, by whom, about removing the body, or about having a postponement?

Witness—I spoke to Nehemiah Burr, and said the body ought not to be moved until a coroner had been called, because I had always heard and always supposed that a body ought not to be moved until the coroner had taken the matter in hand. I did not know but a justice of the peace could act. I knew there was a coroner at South Madison. The day previous I spoke to Mr. Pendelow about a body that had been washed ashore at Madison, and if a coroner was had. When I suggested this to Nehemiah Burr, Mr. Burr thought there could be no harm in moving it to the house. Mr. Stannard came to me and asked me about it, and I told him I thought the body ought not to be moved until seen by a coroner, but as the rest thought differently I acquiesced. Luzerne Stevens, Charles Scranton and myself carried the body. Stevens took hold of the head, Charlie Scranton and myself on either side. I took hold from the shoulder down to the hip. I don't remember that the left shoulder was raised a little as she was found, but that she lay on her back with her head inclined to one side—the right side. I heard no opinion expressed but that it was a case of suicide. I coincided with the rest that it was suicide. The only thing that seemed strange to me was the absence of a knife.

Mr. Waller said there would be no claim but all up there thought at the time it was a case of suicide. Mr. Jones said: Very well.

Witness, continuing—Yes; I helped carry the body down, as has before been stated. There were eight of us. The body was carried down feet foremost. I was at her back—that would—let me see—be on her left-hand side.

Mr. Jones—Do you remember, Mr. Hayden, anything about the pool of blood there?

Witness—I do. I remember that there was blood there, but could not undertake to say how much. The time elapsing before we moved the body was all of three-quarters of an hour. Before we lifted the body to move it, it was so dark that we could not see the ground, and lit matches to look for a knife. We rested the body at the fence of the Stannard house.

Mr. Jones—Give the whole account of what occurred that night in your own words, going slow.

Witness—After a short time Charles Scranton and myself started after a justice of the peace. He said he was going for one, and I said I would go. He came to go as he was the only one that had a horse and wagon there. I went with him. When we got as far as our house, the Hayden house—this house [pointing to the map with pleasantry induced by Mr. Jones's exactness and jocose manner]—I told him I wanted to stop to change my coat. Wife asked me where I was going. I told her, and she said I must stay with her; that she could not stay alone. Yes; Jennie Stevens had gone home, I think. Yes; she knew that I had gone up to the homicide. When Burton Mills said Mary Stannard had her throat cut up on the Brag lot, he being on the road when he said it, Luzerne Stevens's little girl came in and said Mary Stannard had been murdered. The result was that I listened to my wife and remained with her. I told Charlie to stop on the way back for me. About 9 o'clock wife and myself retired to the chamber, and she went to bed and I sat on the bed beside her. The light was in the hallway in full blaze. When Charlie came back he told me he did not see Henry Stone, and that he thought that all who were at the body would be needed at the inquest. There was still no one with my wife but myself. When I heard another carriage come along I went to the window and sang out: "Is that you, Henry?" He said: "Yes." I put my coat and hat on, and went up with him.

Mr. Jones—Do you remember, Mr. Hayden, what was said between you and Mr. Stone?

Witness—I think I said: "Is that you, Henry?" and, he answering yes, I said: "Are you going up to Stannard's?" He said: "Yes." I told him that I helped bring the body down, and asked him if I should be wanted as a witness. He said yes. I went along with him. When we arrived at the house everything seemed to be in confusion. Henry didn't seem to know what was to be done himself, but finally commissioned Charles Scranton and myself to go for a jury. Yes, sir; Mr. Stone had fainted away. Mr. Scranton and myself went to Edward Stannard's, then to Wilbur Stevens's, Edward Stevens's, Austin Stevens's, John Green's, Ellsworth Scranton's, and there were seven in all. We got back at 1 o'clock. Then we lacked five jurymen. Henry Stone said he

would have to go to Durham for a doctor, and would summon the
rest of the jury on the way. It was pitchy dark. I asked Henry if
I could be spared till morning, as I wanted to return to my wife.
He said yes, as I could not be wanted till morning. Went home
and went to bed. Wednesday morning I got up, built the fire ; yes,
5 was my usual hour for getting up, except in winter, when it was 6.
I hitched up my horse to the lumber wagon, and went over to the
wood lot and got a load of wood. I left my house and went here
[on map], drove into the wood lot, commenced to load there [on
map], and then went to the next pile, and so the next, so as to get
the wood the handiest way. I had to take down five or six bars at
three different places on the way. When I intend to come back I
leave these and those down, and put them up on the return. Having got my first load, I went back after a second load. Yes ; I
gave up going to Davis's to work for him, as I had to go to the jury
of inquest. It was at a quarter past 8, perhaps 9, when I got
through with the wood. You ask, if trying to see, how many loads
I could get and draw in one day ? I think about one an hour. The
next thing I did was to change the horse from the lumber wagon to
the buggy, and then take the week's washing over to Talcott
Davis's. It was the ordinary household washing, wife's, mine and
the children's.

Mr. Watrous—Sheets, clothes, etc.? A.—Yes.

Witness—Returning, I took this [showing on map] route to
Stannard's. Got there from half-past 9 to 10 o'clock.

Mr. Jones—You intended to get help for your wife ?

Witness—Well, not at this time—not till when I got home.

Mr. Jones—Very well.

Witness—Returning, I met Andrew Hazlett. I saw that he was
in liquor. I knew that I had met him the night previous up at the
body. I may have asked him if he had come from Stannard's.

Mr. Watrous (politely)—Wait a moment.

Witness—He told me he had just come from the Stannards, but
had stopped at the store—Wilbur Stevens's. I asked him if the
jury had finished their work. He said no. That was all the
conversation I had with Andrew Hazlett. He was in liquor, and I
did not want to converse with him.

Mr. Jones—He (Hazlett) said he asked you if you suspected
anybody. Was there any such conversation ?

Witness—There was not.

Mr. Jones—You call him Andrew Hazen ; did Hazen say to you that they suspected anybody ?   A.—He did not.

Mr. Jones—Was there anything of the kind said ?

Witness—Why, there was nothing of the kind said.

Mr. Watrous—By either ?   A.—By either.

Mr. Jones—Did you suppose his name was Hazen ?

Witness—Yes, sir.   I never heard him called by any other name until after the 3d of September.   Well, I'll mention names, if that's too general, as you say.   There were Luzerne Stevens, Henry Stone, Fillmore Scranton.

Mr. Waller—What we suppose his name was I object to.

Mr. Jones—His name would be to him (witness) what he supposed it was.

Mr. Waller to Mr. Jones—You can argue that when you come to the letter.

Mr. Waller—This man's supposition has no bearing.   What people suppose won't do.   It is right enough to show what other people called him, if they wish ; to show that the girl in writing the letter might have used the name ; but supposition will not do.

Mr. Watrous—There was no doubt of the identity between the man called Hazen and Hazlett.

The court allowed that witness should give the name he knew the man by.

Mr. Watrous—That's all we want.

Witness (emphatically in answer to question)—No ! I never knew him by any other name than Andrew Hazen except till the trial at South Madison, when he said his name was Hazlett.

Mr. Jones—Now go on.

Witness—I saw Susan Hawley as I arrived.   I asked her where the men were.   She said up where the body was found.   I drove home, put up my horse, and went to the spot.   Went back, after a little, to the Stannard house, and then back home and got ready to be at the inquest.   When up in the woods the men said the jury would be at work about 1 o'clock.   I was the first witness called. My testimony was in answers.   Henry E. Stone put every question to me but one, and Edward Stannard put that.   Mr. Stone asked where I first saw Mary Stannard after her return from Guilford ;

when I next saw her; and where I was Tuesday. I was asked where I was Tuesday afternoon. My answer was that I went over to the wood lot. Ed. Stannard asked me if Mary Stannard told me the cause of her trouble, and I answered that she never told me she had any trouble, and therefore I knew not the cause. I, being finished with, asked that my examination be final, as I wished to go and get help for my wife. On my return I found my wife very nervous, and I went and got Mrs. Davis. Mrs. Davis got to the house near 1 o'clock. Mrs. Davis was the lady with my wife during her confinement. She stayed four weeks then.

Mr. Jones—How long were you before the jury of inquest?

Witness—Well, I was going to say five minutes; it may have been ten. It was a very short time. No, sir; I never made the slightest attempt to conceal my visit to Middletown or what I purchased.

Mr. Jones—Mr. Hayden, you may state if you told the court at Madison where you went and what you purchased. Was anything asked about the arsenic except by me?

Witness—I don't remember that there was a single question asked about what I purchased except by you, Mr. Jones.

Mr. Jones—And what did you say, among other things, that you purchased?

Witness—That I bought arsenic. After my arrest, also, as you say, I spoke about it, and before any trial. (To Mr. Waller)—It was Friday September 6.

Mr. Jones—And had you any counsel at that time?

Witness—I had none.

Mr. Jones—Where was it spoken of on that Friday?

Witness—It was spoken of in the probate office in Madison. When I arrived at Madison in the care of Sheriff Hull, I sent for my stewards. Two only could come; they were William Minor and Alexander Johnson. I took them into a little room off from the probate office, and told them of my arrest.

Mr. Waller—Wait a moment. I can't see what this man told confidentially to his friends in a private room on the eve of his arrest, and friends who are of the same society, and what he said to counsel, or what Damon said to Pythias or Pythias to Damon, with the bond of affection existing, has to do with this case. He did not tell publicly so that the authorities could get it.

Mr. Jones said what the next claim the state would make the Lord only knew. Many untenable positions had been taken and dropped by the state. How was Mr. Hayden to tell it? Was he to stand on the steps of the probate office and proclaim it? That was the only way he could make it public until he had an opportunity in court, and then he opened his mouth. If he desired to keep it a secret until forced to disclose it, why then did he tell it before the word arsenic had been mentioned? Friends? Are they not within the reach of a subpœna? Now, we propose to show that on Thursday he told his wife of it, that at South Madison he told of it—before arsenic entered into this case at all.

Mr. Waller—Mr. Jones, do you propose to put the stewards on the stand?

Mr. Jones (decidedly)—I don't propose to tell you, but I do say that when I put in evidence I don't intend to back out of it. (Laughter.)

The court admitted the question.

Witness resumed—I told them (the stewards) of the circumstances of my arrest in the ante-room, and of my movements since I had left Madison Monday noon; told them that I went to Middletown Tuesday morning, what I purchased there, and what purchases I made at Madison.

Mr. Jones—State whether you heard of "quick medicine" being purchased?

Witness—I had. It was on Friday I was arrested at 5 o'clock. I was washing myself and wiping my face when the sheriff came in. Yes; the purchase of arsenic was told at the house of William Minor, one of my stewards, at the dinner table. Mr. Minor, his wife, the boy, my wife, and, I think, another lady, were at the table, and myself. This was Monday, September 9. In the evening I spoke of it in the presence of Mr. and Mrs. Minor and daughter, my wife, and Mrs. Talcott Davis. I think it was in the parlor at Mr. Minor's. I don't recall it this moment that I spoke of it to any others. Yes; I met Duell Stevens on Wednesday, whom I met while in Middletown. I think he was going to Northford, and was changing his horse for the object. I have an indistinct recollection of asking him where he was going. He said he was going to notify some friends of the Stannard family of the death of Mary Stannard.

MR. HAYDEN'S ROCKLAND RESIDENCE IN WINTER.

[Showing the barn where the "barn arsenic" was deposited.]

PHOTO ENG CO. N.Y.

Mr. Jones—Mr. Hayden, when did you know that anybody suspected you ?

Witness—Wednesday afternoon. Upon leaving the jury room I returned home, and found that Mrs. Davis had consented to stay with my wife until next day. I then went to the Stannard house. I was on the road in front of the Stannard house, and a gentleman from Middlefield, Valentine Miller, drove up and spoke to me. He was an acquaintance. I had known him—oh, for four or five years. Had not known his name but two. He informed me that Dr. Matthewson had reported through Durham and Middlefield that Mary Stannard, who was at work for Hayden, had been found with her throat cut in a lot opposite Hayden's house ; that she was in the family way ; that Hayden had got himself into a scrape and couldn't preach any more for years. That was the substance of what he told me. I was informed later in the day by Talcott Davis— [Objected to. Mr. Jones argued.]

Witness—Mr. Davis told me that Susan Hawley—

Mr. Waller—I object.

Mr. Jones—Well, Mr. Hayden, state if informed by Talcott Davis that it was said you had purchased " quick medicine ? "

Witness—I was.

Mr. Jones—And where ? A.—At Middletown.

Mr. Jones—Were you informed what Susan Hawley had testified to by Mr. Davis ? A.—I was.

Mr. Jones—Were you informed when you would be arrested ?

Witness—No, sir ; I can't say that I was, but that it was an impression that I would be arrested next day. Don't think General Wilcox (the Middletown ex-chief of police) told me anything of the kind. Talcott Davis talked with me on this matter just before night.

Mr. Jones—Do you know a man named Richard Eldridge ?

Witness—Yes, sir.

Mr. Jones—Did he see you about it ? A.—Yes, sir.

Mr. Jones—When was that ?

Witness—That was Wednesday afternoon.

[The court took a recess. The prisoner returned to a seat by his wife, and Judge Wilcox, of Madison, who acquitted Mr. Hayden at the first hearing, engaged Mr. Hayden in an animated conversation. Mr. Hayden joined in with spirit. Mr. Hayden, father of the accused, also the mother, sat near. Both are frequently remarked as a nice, elegant-looking elderly couple, and they seem to have the sympathy of all who see them. Various other gentlemen, apparently of some prominence and influence, came up and shook the prisoner very warmly and cordially by the hand, and engaged him in conversation, the prisoner standing up and talking with them in a lively way, and as if much pleased to see them.]

Mr. Jones asked Mr. Hayden when he first informed his wife that he was suspected?

Witness—Thursday morning. I knew it the evening before, but put it off so that she could have a good night's rest. I told her in the middle of the afternoon. It was up-stairs.

Mr. Jones—Mr. Hayden (impressively), what was the effect upon your wife?

Mr. Waller—What is the object of that?

Mr. Jones (gravely and solemnly)—Simply to show that it is a wonder that this poor woman remembered anything of that day's events, such was her condition.

The Court—Well, make the inquiry.

Witness, in a low voice—She broke completely down. When I had broken the news to her she seemed broken. She was not able to stand up. She was extremely nervous. She was not able to sit up at all that day. I told her what Mr. Miller had told me, what Mr. Davis had told me about the "quick medicine." I sat down and told her of my trip to Middletown, and all that occurred. I was arrested on Friday morning and taken to South Madison. I next saw my wife Sunday night. The matter was talked over then.

Mr. Jones (impressively)—Mr. Hayden! You have said you were never criminally intimate with Mary Stannard. I desire to ask you, were you ever much in her company?

Witness—I was not.

Mr. Jones—Will you tell us about it?

Witness—She came first in 1877 to take care of the children while my wife was teaching school, and she helped about the house, returning after school to her home. I was working on the farm. She came in the latter part of April. Yes; Mary was there while I was away, and was at her home while I was at home.

Mr. Jones (impressively)—Mr. Hayden, has there ever been any kind of intimacy between you and Mary Stannard beside that proper to exist between employer and employed ?

Witness—There has not.

Mr. Jones—Have you ever been walking with that girl on any occasion in any lot or field ? A.—I never was.

Mr. Hayden gave the three occasions when he took Mary Stannard riding, as his wife had said ; once to get cherries at Davis's, the family being along ; again taking her home when her face was poisoned, and by his wife's wish ; and again and lastly to Middletown by his wife's wish, so that Mary could make some little purchases at the stores there, as had been promised her by Mrs. Hayden. On the trip to Middletown I hitched my horse at a point opposite Mr. Tyler's drug store. I don't think we were in Middletown over an hour. Went into no house or building of any kind with her. She would occasionally bring her purchases and lay them in the wagon. She finally said she wished to buy some cups and saucers for Susan, and she said she knew of a store, and she walked to it and I drove up. I stopped at the store and waited for her, and she bought what she wanted. On the way that day I stopped at Burton's about the tools. On the way saw Luzerne Stevens and his wife.

Mr. Jones—With the exception of those three times, was she ever in your carriage ?

Witness (with some emphasis)—Not to my knowledge. Certainly never with me.

Mr. Jones—Have you ever met her in your cow pasture ?

Witness described location of lot, and said in answer to a question of Mr. Jones, if he had ever seen Mary at the pasture lot or by the spring, that he never had, emphasizing never somewhat.

Mr. Jones, now showing the knife, asked if witness had ever met with a mishap in using it in carpentering ?

Witness—I did. The small blade was the sharpest. I always intended to have a keen edge on the little blade so as to make a distinct mark in drawing it across a board when using a try-square. I cut myself with it while at work on a well-curb in the barn a week before the child was born. The rafters bothered me. I wanted to put a pole in the center. I whirled the pole around, and it shut down on the blade, and shut it up and caught my finger, cutting it. The scar can be seen now. It is the scar I showed to the jury the other day. Yes; it was cut very deeply. It was, I should judge, from five-eighths to three-quarters of an inch long. Yes; my boy carried the knife. He has had it very often. I let him have it, as I would rather any one would cut themselves with a sharp knife than a dull one. It does not tear the flesh so much. The boy had cut his finger with it.

Mr. Jones—Mr. Hayden, did you have any money with you when you went to Middletown with Mary?

Witness—I did; three cents.   [Laughter.]

Mr. Jones—Not any more?

Witness (with some emphasis and a laugh,—That was every cent I had. Yes; I could have borrowed some from my church people. The society then owed me fifty dollars.

Mr. Jones—Mr. Hayden, at the time of your arrest do you remember what there was in your barn?

Witness—I do.   There was my horse, buggy, cow, twelve bunches of shingles. The shingles lay just east of the post where I hitched my horse. I had also a pile of matched boards, which were piled up east and west. In the northeast corner of the barn were six or eight chestnut planks. I had two harnesses and pieces of harness, a bundle of shavings, an old lounge, an old running gear of a wagon and an old clothes-horse. These were on the barn floor. In the south part of the barn were two kinds of hay. On top of the hay were my hay rigging and two or three boards. On the scaffolding in the north part were a corn sheller, two small grind-stones, two scythe snaths, two rakes and two pitchforks. One of the pitchforks was a short mow-fork, and the other was a long fork. I had a three-tined fork, but that was at Stannard's. On the girths were a curry comb and brush, three or four bottles, one being a quart bottle containing horse liniment. This girth was about six feet from the floor. There were also wooden boxes that had formerly contained bolts. There were strips of iron; an old cross-cut saw on the east stringer. There were a large number of traps of one kind or another.

Mr. Jones—What was the width of your barn floor, Mr. Hayden?

Witness—It was ten feet, I think. I have always called the barn 18 by 36, but its exact measurement was 17¾ by 35½.

Mr. Jones—Was there anything in that barn that would reach from the scaffolding across to the mow?

Witness—There was not, and never had been to my knowledge

Mr. Jones—What was the size of the shed adjoining the barn?

Witness—It was just large enough to run under my farm wagon and business wagon. I always kept my top buggy on the barn floor.

Mr. Jones—Mr. Hayden, where had you been two weeks prior to this homicide?

Witness—I made preparations to go to Martha's Vineyard on the 17th of August. This was on Saturday. I preached in Madison on Sunday, and on the following Monday went to the Vineyard and remained one week. I returned a week earlier than I expected to, on account of the illness of my wife.

Mr. Jones inquired of witness if he thought of anything further than was mentioned that he desired to say.

Witness said there was nothing except a few words in explanation of the arrangement he made about purchasing the Hayden place, so called. He then explained briefly about the arrangement with Mr. Scranton, the owner.

Mr. Jones—You may take the witness, gentlemen.

His Cross-examination by the State.

The cross-examination was conducted by Mr. Waller for the State.

Mr. Waller—I understand you, Mr. Hayden, to deny all the allegations made against you in regard to your intimacy with Mary Stannard?

Witness—I do so, most emphatically.

Mr. Waller—You have stated that you said at the Stannard house, on your return, on the 3d of September, that you had been to Middletown, did you not?

Witness—I think I did.

Mr. Waller—You did not tell it in a secret, confidential manner?

Witness—No, sir.

Mr. Waller—It is not strange that Susan Hawley said she heard you say it, is it?

Witness—She could have heard it had she been out of doors, but she was not. Only Mary and Benjamin Stevens were out of doors when I rode up.

Mr. Waller—Now give me your profound attention. I desire to read you a series of questions and your answers as you gave them in the hearing at Madison. Did you say in your evidence at Madison that you did not remember of saying that when you got to Stannard's you did not recollect of saying where you had been?

Witness—I don't remember this question or answer.

Mr. Waller—Did you not say that you did not say anything about being to Durham, or what you had got?

Witness—I don't remember this question.

Mr. Waller—Did you swear at Madison that you did not tell anybody that you had been to Durham or Middletown?

Witness—I don't remember that the question was put to me in that way.

Mr. Watrous asked the privilege of addressing the court. He said he desired to inquire if this line of examination was correct and legitimate. Is it right to ask this witness if this or that question was asked him at Madison? How can it be expected that he can remember a long series of questions read to him from a paper. I have heard this style of questioning rebuked by the court, and I think it should be done in this case.

Mr. Waller said he had asked such questions as he was advised were asked at that hearing, and had given the answers as he was advised they were given at that trial at Madison. Now, if the witness told the people at the Stannard house that he had been to Middletown, then it weaves together the story told by Susan Hawley of Mary Stannard and the "quick" medicine.

Mr. Watrous replied briefly. He said he bid the attorneys God speed in their declaration that they had "got a clew to the unsolving of the Susan Hawley riddle." He thought, however, that it was unfair to make such flings at his client.

The judges consulted briefly. Judge Park said they did not understand that the counsel claimed to use the exact phraseology that was used on the former trial. They thought it was proper to inquire what the witness testified to on the former trial.

Mr. Waller—Did you not state at Madison that you did not have any conversation with Mary Stannard about your going to Middletown?

Witness—I don't recollect what I said at that time.

Mr. Waller—Where did you see Mary Stannard on that morning?

Witness—I saw Mary and Benjamin Stevens leaning on the fence.

Mr. Waller—Did you talk with Mary Stannard, except to say good morning? A.—I did not.

Mr. Waller—Was she in a position so that you could have talked with her privately if you had desired?

Witness—No, sir; I think not.

Mr. Waller—Do you think she was in a position so you could have given her a sign to go to the spring?

Witness—I think not.

Mr. Waller—Could she, while leaving the house to go to the spring, have given you any sign without it being noticed by those present? A.—I think not.

Mr. Waller—About how long did you have Mary Stannard in your eye before you stopped your carriage near the spring?

Witness—But a moment or two.

Mr. Waller—How near full of water was the pail which Mary brought from the spring?

Witness—I should think it was nearly even full.

Mr. Waller—How much would the pail hold?

Witness—I should think ten or twelve quarts.

Mr. Waller—Would it have been any trouble for Mary to have passed you the pail, while you were sitting in the carriage?

Witness—I think it would, from my position in the buggy.

Mr. Waller here produced a tin pail (holding about eight quarts), and asked if the pail that Mary had was any larger than that.

Witness—I should think it was.

Mr. Waller—Was not that the identical pail?

Witness—I cannot tell, Mr. Waller. My impression is that it was a larger pail than that.

Mr. Waller—Do you think it would have been difficult for her to have handed you this pail if it had been full of water?

Witness—I think it would, under the circumstances.

Mr. Waller—How long were you out of that carriage?

Witness—It might have been a minute; perhaps not half a minute.

Mr. Waller—When you were out of the carriage would you have had time to say this: "I have been to Middletown, have got quick medicine, meet me at the Big Rock at 3 o'clock"?

Mr. Jones objected to this question. He said it was evident that the state desired to convey to the minds of the jury that this was just the question asked by the witness.

Mr. Waller said the object was to find out how long the witness was there. The court ruled out the question.

Mr. Waller—How long were you, in minutes, out of that carriage?

Witness—I don't think exceeding one minute.

Mr. Waller—How near were you to the carriage when you jumped out?

MARY E. STANNARD.

[From a photograph taken shortly before her death.]

Witness—I was close by the wheel. Mary stood within a foot of me.

Mr. Waller—Did Mary go towards home after giving you the water?

Witness—I don't know. I said thank you, and jumped into my carriage and drove home.

Mr. Waller—You say you did not know when you met Mary where the "Big Rock" was?

Witness—I did not. I had never heard of "Big Rock," "Fox Ledge," or "Whippoorwill Rock," at that time.

Mr. Waller—Is not this "Big Rock" as famous in Rockland as is East Rock in New Haven? A.—It may be now. (Laughter.)

Mr. Waller—Did you have any reason to know on this day that Mary knew where this "Big Rock" was? A.—No, sir

Mr. Waller—Do you know of anybody in Rockland that had any arsenic in their house on the 3d of September but yourself?

Witness—I do not.

Mr. Waller—When was the last conversation you had with your wife about poison for rats before the 3d of September?

Witness—I should say it was in the last week in August.

Mr. Waller—You had been talking about poisoning the rats with "ratsbane" seven or eight months before this, had you?

Witness—Yes, sir.

Mr. Waller—When was it that you talked with your church stewards about poison for killing rats?

Witness—I think it was on August 1

Mr. Waller—Had you gone into Mr. Meigs's store at South Madison between the 11th of August and the 3d of September, and purchased arsenic, don't you think he would have known you?

Witness—Yes, sir.

Mr. Waller—Did you not know that Mr. Meigs kept an apothecary shop? A.—I did not.

Mr. Waller—Did you ever inquire of Mr. Meigs for arsenic or Paris green? A.—No, sir.

Mr. Waller—Did you expect to put the arsenic in the cellar to kill the rats at night, and then take it away in the morning, or what there was left? A.—No, sir.

Mr. Waller—Did you expect to use the arsenic without letting your wife know it until afterward?

Witness—I did not intend that she should know it until the rats were dead.

Mr. Waller—What time in the day on September 3 did you make up your mind to buy arsenic ?

Witness—I don't think I decided to buy it on that day until I reached Durham.

Mr. Waller—Did you, on the night before going, contemplate going to Middletown ?

Witness—I did not ; I only thought of going to Durham.

Mr. Waller—Did you stop at Durham going out ?

Witness—No, sir.

Mr. Waller—Did you know whether arsenic was kept in Durham ?

Witness—I did not, as I had never inquired.

Mr. Waller—Did you have any motive in going to Middletown except to get your tools ?

Witness—That was the principal object.

[A recess was ordered at this point. After recess, which continued nearly an hour, the cross-examination of Mr. Hayden was continued.]

Mr. Waller—I will ask you, sir, in going to Durham, which road did you take ?

Witness—I took the right-hand road.

Mr. Waller—When were you spoken to about fullers' earth ?

Witness—On that morning my wife spoke to me about it. She may have spoken about it before.

Mr. Waller—Where did you get fullers' earth before the 3d of September?

Witness—It may have been three months before. I then got it at Tyler's in Middletown.

Mr. Waller—How many times during the year, between September, 1877, and September, 1878, had you purchased fullers' earth ?

Witness—I cannot tell positively.

Mr. Waller—Had you purchased fullers' earth at Durham ?

Witness—I had not. I was not aware that I could get it.

Mr. Waller—When your wife spoke to you about getting fullers' earth, why did you not tell her that you did not know as you should go where you could get it.

Witness—I don't know why I did not.

Mr. Waller—You don't know that fuller's-earth was used at Durham. Don't you know, as a minister who was around among the families of his parish, that fullers' earth was generally used on babies?

Witness—I was not in the habit of examining the babies to see whether the powder was used or not. (Laughter.)

Mr. Waller—Did you not suppose that the tools you were in search of at Mr. Burton's in Middletown were at the Industrial School?

Witness—I may have thought so. Mrs. Burton told me in August that the tools were at the school.

Mr. Waller—What time did you get to Burton's on the 3d of September? A.—I think about 8 o'clock.

Mr. Waller—How long were you living in Middletown?

Witness—I was there from September, 1873, to April, 1875.

Mr. Waller—Could you see the Industrial School or any portion of it from the college grounds?

Witness—I don't know, but I think not.

Mr. Waller—How far would you have to go from the house where you lived in Middletown so that you could see the Industrial School buildings?

Witness—Perhaps thirty rods.

Mr. Waller—Did you not drive right by the Industrial School buildings?

Witness—I did, I think, about two years before.

Mr. Waller—You were disappointed in not getting the tools at Burton's, were you not?

Witness—I may say yes.

Mr. Waller—Now, can you tell us the reason you did not go to the Industrial School for those tools?

Witness—One reason was that an agreement was made that the tools should be left at Burton's house, and another reason was that I did not know exactly where the Industrial School was.

Mr. Waller—Could you not have asked Mrs. Burton where the Industrial School was?

Witness—I suppose I could, but I did not think it necessary.

Mr. Waller—Now, if you had got those tools that day, and had taken them home, your wife would have known that you had been to Middletown, would she not?

Witness—Undoubtedly she would.

Mr. Waller—Now, if it had not been for the feed for the horse, you probably would not have gone to Middletown on that day, would you? A.—Probably not.

Mr. Waller—Why did you not get your feed at South Madison on Monday, instead of going to Durham?

Witness—One reason was that I had no store account at Madison, and another that I had to pay more.

Mr. Waller—Did you not testify at Madison that your reason was that you could not get credit?

Witness—I don't think I did.

Mr. Waller—Were you aware that you could not get trusted at South Madison?

Witness—The reason I thought I could not was because there had been trouble with Mr. Hull, the storekeeper, and a previous minister, about pay, and Mr. Hull and his father, the sheriff, had said that there would be no more trusting Methodist ministers. (Laughter.)

Mr. Waller—Did you not return a bag to Mr. Hull's store in which there had been feed that you had purchased?

Witness—I did. I bought the feed when I was teaching at Madison, and paid cash for it.

Mr. Waller—How long had you been a customer of David Tyler of Middletown? A.—Since 1873.

Mr. Waller—How many purchases did you make at Mr. David Tyler's during any one year?

Witness—I cannot say. I used to purchase my tobacco there and other articles.

Mr. Waller—When you went into the store on that day (September 3) do you think that David Tyler knew your name or your occupation?

Witness—I cannot tell certainly.

Mr. Waller—At Middletown did you get an ounce of arsenic?

Witness—I did. It was put up in ordinary white paper. I cannot tell exactly how big the package was.

Mr. Waller—Will you take a piece of paper and fold it as near as you can to the size of the package?

[Witness folded a piece of paper and handed it to Mr. Waller, and said it was as near the size as he could recollect.]

Mr. Waller—Was the arsenic in your pocket after you got home, and when you went into the house ? A.—No, sir.

Mr. Waller—Where was it ?

Witness—I took it out of my pocket and put it under the seat of my carriage before going into the house. After taking other things into the house, I got the tin box in the kitchen and put the arsenic into it for safety. I don't know, but I think the wrapper and envelope and string about the arsenic were thrown into the shavings barrel in the barn.

Mr. Waller—Did it occur to you that the children might get the paper and be poisoned by it ?

Witness—I don't think they could have reached the paper, as the barrel was nearly empty.

Mr. Waller—Now, can you tell us whether that paper and that string around that arsenic was ever seen by mortal man after you removed it ?

Witness—I cannot say positively.

Mr. Waller—Had you put that arsenic down on a stringer, in the paper, would it not have been just as safe as it was in the tin box ?

Witness—It might have been, but I was always in the habit of putting such articles in boxes after purchasing them. I did intend to use some of the arsenic, the night after I bought it, upon the rats. I don't know, Mr. Waller, that there was any more special reason why I should use it that night on the rats than any other. I had to get up on the hay to put the arsenic on the stringer of the barn. Climbed up to it on my carriage. I put it on the stringer. There was hay on the stringer, but nothing else to my knowledge. The hay concealed the box.

Mr. Waller—If you had expected to use it so soon, why put it away so carefully, with such precaution ? You deemed it necessary, did you ? A.—Yes, sir.

Mr. Waller—Nobody saw you put it there ?

Witness—I don't know, sir. I didn't see my children around. It was not an extraordinary occurrence for me to climb up on the carriage in the barn. The barn faces the road thirty-six feet. The doors are ten feet wide. [The prisoner answered without confusion or discomfiture, except manifesting sometimes uneasiness, and answered carefully and thoughtfully; yet readily. His face looked heated and much as if his nervous system was keenly alive, but he bore the gaze of three hundred pairs of eyes as well as probably most men could under the circumstances. He held his right hand out before him, the ends of the fingers touching the rail before him, and the fingers were kept moving.]

Mr. Waller—Why didn't you use the arsenic the next morning? Is there any reason?

Witness—I think there is. I was called away.

Mr. Waller—Not till after you had done your chores?

Witness—No, sir.

Mr. Waller—Is there any reason—special reason—why you did not get and use the arsenic that morning?

Witness—Yes ; I didn't get the time. I was busy. I went also after the wood.

Mr. Waller—Was there nothing the next morning that led you to think that you were suspected ? A.—There was not.

Mr. Waller—It did not enter into your mind to tell anybody during that day that you had bought arsenic?

Witness—Why, no ; it was nobody's business.

Mr. Waller—It didn't occur to you to tell them at the coroner's inquest about it?

Witness—I was not asked about it.

Mr. Waller—It didn't enter your mind that you were suspected?

Witness—No, sir ; it didn't enter my mind.

Mr. Waller—You were up at the body? The general opinion was that it was suicide? A.—Yes, sir.

Mr. Waller—You coincided with them? A.—Yes, sir.

Mr. Waller—When you suggested a coroner, everybody then thought it was suicide, did they?

Witness—I heard no other opinion expressed.

Mr. Jones—Why is that? How can he know what everybody thought?

Mr. Waller—Everybody that he heard.

Mr. Waller—And then about having a doctor. Was there not some reason you gave for going home?

Witness—Yes, sir ; my going for a doctor would detain me too long from my wife.

Mr. Waller—And you went home and slept that night?

Witness—I did.

Mr. Waller.—You still did not know you were suspected?

Witness—I had no reason to think so.

Mr. Waller—When the juror asked you that question, when you last saw Mary and where you had been that afternoon of the homicide, did you not think they were suspecting you?

Mr. Jones—You assume some of the questions.

Mr. Waller—I mean to mention those he testified to.

Mr. Waller—You say Hazlett, or the man you called Hazen, was in liquor when you met him in the morning.   Witness—Yes.

Mr. Waller—And have you said all he said?

Witness—I think I have.

Mr. Waller—Now I'll ask if there was anything in the answers of that man—what did you ask him?

Witness—I asked if the coroner's jury had completed their work, and he said no, and said where he had been.

Mr. Waller—Was there anything like intoxication in his answers?

Witness—But he showed by his manner, Mr. Waller.   No, sir, had he said more, I think I should have remembered it.

Mr. Waller—Now, sir, did you at that time that Mrs. Luzerne Stevens and the people in that house opposite your house testified before the coroner's jury the time you left the house; did you hear them?

Question repeated at request.

Witness—No, sir ; did not know that the neighbors knew when I left the house.   I do swear that I did not testify at the coroner's jury that I left the house at 1:15 o'clock.   There was not a note taken of the evidence while I was there.   No, sir, I did not tell them that I left at a quarter past one.   That would not be the truth. Yes, sir, I told at Madison the time I left the house.

Mr. Waller—When, at Madison, you fixed the time in your testimony, did you know that Luzerne Stevens had sworn differently?

Witness—I knew that he had testified that I left the house at 2 o'clock.

Mr. Waller—Now, sir, when in Middletown that day, did you see Dr. Bailey?   A.—I did.   I heard him testify at Madison.

Mr. Waller—Did you contradict the testimony of Dr. Bailey as to what was said between you?   (Objected to, and answer given in another form.)

Witness—I did.   I have not notes of his evidence.

Mr. Jones objected.   No inference should be drawn against the defendant that he did not arise in court—which he would have no right to do—and declare Dr. Bailey's testimony false.

Mr. Waller—My question is, did you hear Dr. Bailey testify at Madison as to what passed between you at Middletown?

Mr. Watrous—Let's get that question down.

Mr. Waller—I will waive it for a moment. Did you meet Dr. Bailey in Middletown? A.—I did.

Mr. Waller—Did you talk with him at that time about diseases peculiar to women?

An argument ensued between counsel, Mr. Watrous objecting that no evidence in chief before the court had been had on this point.

Mr. Waller said he wished to find if the accused had talked with the doctor in relation to diseases peculiar to women. Objection withdrawn.

Mr. Waller—Did you converse with him about diseases peculiar to women, or about menstruation during pregnancy, or as to the condition of a certain woman whose condition you had a right to know while she was pregnant?

Witness—Will you repeat your question, Mr. Waller?

Mr. Waller—Did you ask about diseases peculiar to women during pregnancy?

Witness—I think I can say as to that that I did.

Mr. Waller—Did you inform the Doctor that your wife had been confined? A.—I did.

Mr. Waller—Did you hear Dr. Bailey's testimony at Madison with reference to what passed between you?

Mr. Jones told witness that he needn't answer.

Mr. Waller said it was to show that witness heard the doctor testify at Madison and did not contradict him. Now he (counsel) wished to ask witness if he would contradict the doctor's statement.

Mr. Waller—Was the conversation with Dr. Bailey as to the possibility of menstruation during periods of pregnancy? A.—It was.

Mr. Waller—Did you know before you had this conversation that your wife was irregular in pregnancy?

Witness—Yes, sir. That was the first child. My wife was declared pregnant during menstruation by Dr. Bailey, who was called to decide, she having illness peculiar to women. The doctor first asked me, not I him, if she had been troubled with this child as when with the other, born at East Greenwich. I asked, "Do you have many such cases?"

Mr. Waller—Did you ask him if all women might be pregnant and have their discharges? A.—No. sir.

Mr. Waller now asked about the wood-lot, and said he knew witness would not use his horse ill, and asked him about the picking up of wood, and if he could not have gone without getting wood that day.

Witness said that Mondays he was tired from his Sundays' work, and if chips were in the house they would answer for fire. I went to get the feed because I wanted it for the horse. I went for oats, because I wanted the oats the most.

Mr. Waller—You say you worked continuously at the wood lot for an hour and a half?

Witness—I said I kept at work all the time. I do not remember that I sat down. No, sir; do not know that anybody saw me going into the wood-lot, or coming out of it. I only know that my wife testified to seeing me by the Burr barn.

Mr. Jones—Nothing strange that he should be seen in Rockland.

Mr. Waller—Now, sir, your horse, a nervous, restless kind of a horse, was it, and you were afraid of horse-flies, and couldn't you have tied him?

Witness—No, sir; there was but one tree large enough to hitch him to, and at the foot of that it was swampy and no place to hitch a horse.

Mr. Waller—More flies and cross ones in that swamp than anywhere else? A.—I won't say that. (Spectators laughed.)

Mr. Waller—You say you met Hazen, or Hazlett, on your return, and that various people called him Hazlett?

Witness—Yes. Luzerne Stevens, Henry Stone and Wilbur Stevens called him by that name. I cannot state the time when either of them so called him.

Mr Waller—Did you ever call him Hazen?

Witness—I cannot say, but I can say this—

Mr. Waller—Answer my question.

Mr. Jones to witness—You will have a chance by and by.

Mr Waller—Before you testified at Madison, had you heard a theory that a certain name on a certain letter was Hazen? (Witness asked for information.)

Mr. Waller gave answer about the letter, and the supposition about the name Hazen.

Mr. Jones—We never claimed Hazen ; it was Hazlett.

Mr. Waller—Ah! I'll recollect it. I thought they called it Hazen.

Witness said : I never heard the suggestion at all that the name was Hazen or Hazlett in the letter.

Mr. Waller—Did you testify at Madison that Davis met you in the swamp and rode home with you? A.—No, sir, I did not. (Mr. Waller read Madison evidence.)

Witness—I don't recollect of so testifying.

Mr. Waller—Now, when you got home from the wood-lot it was about 4 ?

Witness—Yes, sir ; and then picked up chips, and then changed my clothes.

Mr. Waller—Did your wife see you when you got back from the wood-lot before you changed your clothes? A.—She did.

Mr. Waller—Ah! she did. You told us there was a peddler down-stairs while you were changing your clothes. Was he there while you were changing your clothes ?

Witness—A part of the time. Wife was down-stairs all the time while I was changing my clothes. I don't recollect about changing my shoes. Think I took them off before going up stairs. The shirt I took off was the one I wore to Middletown.

Mr. Waller—Were you in a state of perspiration ?

Witness—Yes, I perspired pretty freely. I always perspire very easily.

[The Court took a recess. Mr. Hayden resumed sitting with his wife, and engaged in cheerful conversation with her. Mrs. Hayden, however, broke down, and cried with many tears, and Mr. Hayden seemed unable to comfort her, but was at last successful. Spectators visiting the court-room remarked that they were agreeably surprised in the prisoner, and credited him with a pleasing voice and every indication of frankness and truthfulness.]

Mr. Waller—Did you tell us, sir, that you didn't know where your wife stood when you brought in the oysters and the knife ?

Witness—I said that I could not name it. I said I handed the knife to wife. I do not know where she stood then, except that it was in the kitchen. I did say how I held it.

Mr. Waller—Will you be good enough to show how you held that knife?

Witness—I will, sir; if you will be good enough to get me the knife. (Sheriff brought the knife, and witness took the pail and showed how.)

Mr. Waller—What fixes it so distinctly how you held that knife?

Witness—My hands were slimy with the oysters.

Mr. Waller—Slimy? A.—Yes, sir; they were slimy. I do not recollect where she stood. I gave it to her. [Mr. Waller read from stenographic notes of first trial, in which it was said that he, witness, did not remember exactly what he did with it; whether he put it on the table, shelf, or handed it to his wife.]

Mr. Waller—Is there a good reason why you should recollect it now when you couldn't then?

Witness—Yes, sir; I have a very good reason.

Mr. Waller—Well, keep it to yourself now.

Mr. Waller—Do you know of any other family that has a jack-knife to peel pears with? A.—I don't know.

Mr. Waller—Was there any reason that you know of that the common case-knife would not do as well to peel those pears with?

Witness—I did not peel the pears. A case-knife is extremely unhandy to handle in peeling the pears. [Shown one of the family case-knives.]

Mr. Waller—Were the case-knives in as good condition for peeling pears as this one? A.—I can't say.

Mr Waller—Did anybody hear you except your wife when she asked you to leave it home to peel pears with?

Witness—No one but the children. That knife I bought of the postmaster at South Madison.

Mr Waller—What did you pay for it? A.—The price was seventy-five cents. I got it for sixty. (Spectators laughed.)

Mr. Waller.—Was there reason for the discount?

Witness—He gave it to me cheaper because I was a minister.

Mr. Waller—Now, sir, did anybody else in Rockland see you using that knife?

Witness—I can't say. So far as I know, all the inhabitants of Rockland may have seen me using it.

Mr. Waller—Now, sir, if that knife had been found near the body you would have known it, of course. A.—I think I should.

Mr. Waller—Do you think the man who sold you the knife would remember it?

Witness—I can't say. Don't think he would. I don't know his habit of memory.

Mr. Waller—Was there no knife there at the body?

Witness—We saw none.

Mr. Waller—Now, sir, the knife has been used for a variety of purposes—killing chickens, cutting beef, etc. Do you ever know of its being used in connection with a dog? A.—I do not.

Mr. Waller—So that if dog's blood got on it, you have no knowledge of it? A.—No, sir.

Mr. Waller—In the presence of Mrs. Talcott Davis, her daughter and your wife, you asked for your knife, and were not able to answer what you wanted it for?

Witness—I was not asked such a question, Mr. Waller.

Mr. Waller—Now where was that knife found Wednesday noon?

Witness—It was on the shelf over the wood-box. It was one of the proper places, yes, sir; to look for it. Did not know then when it was put there. I think I wanted it that noon to clean my finger-nails with, but I don't recollect it exactly. I was dressing to go up to Stannard's. I have sometimes cleaned it after using it. I did not clean it before going away. The smaller blade was the sharper.

Mr. Waller—You said you would rather have your little boy cut himself with a sharp knife than a dull one. Why?

Witness—Because it makes a cleaner cut. For just the same reason that I would rather run a sharp nail into my foot than a dull one.

Mr. Waller (Solemnly—Was that knife in a proper condition for a clean cut? A.—That I can't say.

Mr. Waller—You had no improper connection with Mary Stannard? A.—*Never!*

Mr. Waller—You were at the oyster supper in March, 1878?

Witness—I was. Got home with my wife about 1 o'clock. Mary Stannard was taking care of the children.

Mr. Waller—Was anybody at your house that night except the children and Mary? A.—Don't know.

Mr. Waller—Did you leave the house more than once.

Witness—Only once.

Mr. Waller—Were you at the oyster supper at 11 o'clock?

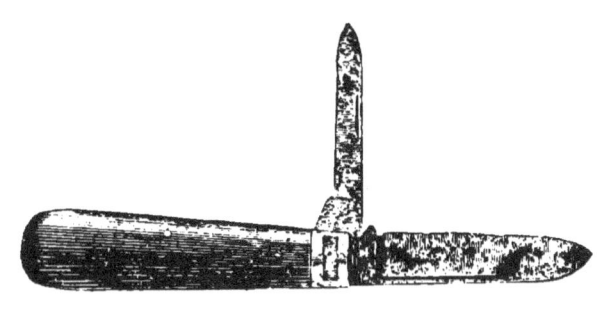

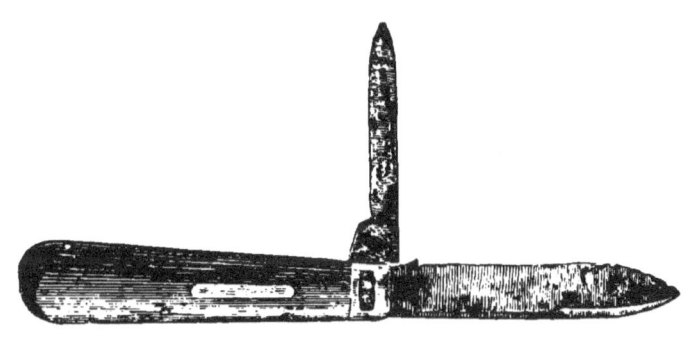

THE KNIVES IN THE CASE.

[The small knife is Mr. Hayden's ; the other was found near the scene of the tragedy, and the owner has never been discovered.]

Witness—I was.

Mr. Waller—Did you see Charles Hawley and Imogene Stannard that night at some other place than the oyster supper?

Witness—Do not know.

Mr. Waller—Were they not at your house? A.—Cannot say.

Mr. Waller asked a long question as to the matter under consideration.

Witness asked for a repetition. Mr. Waller said, why?

Witness—You ask so many questions; you say you, and then I; I can't answer directly yes or no; not the way you state it.

Mr. Waller—Well, I will reconstruct and ask each separately. Were you in your house after 11 o'clock? A.—Yes, sir.

Mr. Waller—Did they, in your presence, ask that Mary Stannard might go home? A.—They did not.

Mr. Waller—Were you not alone with Mary? A.—No, sir.

Mr. Waller—Well, I've been over it, and the grammar is correct.

Witness—And the answer is correct.

Mr. Waller—Well, sir, you went riding with Mary—I don't mean in any improper sense—alone, three times?

Witness—Twice I was with her alone.

Mr. Waller—Now, it's to the trip to Middletown I wish to direct your attention. Your wife had promised in March—

Witness—It was in February.

Mr. Waller—Oh, the promise was not fulfilled till August?

Witness—No, sir.

Mr. Waller—Ah, now Mary in August stepped in and asked your wife about going to Middletown? A.—Yes.

Mr. Waller—How near were you to Mary?

Witness—I was out doors.

Mr. Waller—Didn't you get into the house before it was arranged?

Witness—No, sir; Mrs. Davis came to the door and called me in.

Mr. Waller—Did you suggest to your wife to have the trip?

Witness—No, sir.

Mr. Waller—On that drive you had no companion carriage—no carriage with you or ahead of you?

Witness—No, sir; don't remember of any.

Mr. Waller—Don't you drive through shady places, groves, over hills and pleasant places on that road?

Witness—Don't remember pleasant places.

Mr. Waller—Through groves?

Witness—We go by hills by the woodside.

Mr. Waller—Well, sir, were you not alone, without sight of any-body, for half hours at a time?

Witness—Well, I presume I was.

Mr. Waller—Very well. You had no familiarity with her?

Witness—Not in the least.

Mr. Waller—Now, you drove your cow to that pasture?

Witness—There (showing on map the spring.

Mr. Waller—Then the spring is above. It is nearly equal distance, isn't it, between Stannard's house and yours?

Witness—It is nearer Stannard's than mine.

Mr. Waller—That's the spring where the Stannards got the water for the family? A.—Yes.

Mr. Waller—Mary usually got the water?

Witness—Well, I can't say that.

Mr. Waller—You've seen her there, haven't you? A.—No, sir.

Mr. Waller—About this spring in summer time the foliage is pretty dense?

Witness—More or less dense off in this direction (pointing to map).

Mr. Waller—Yes, I remember the place, sir; but, off by the spring, is it not a solitary place? I mean that one can go there and not be seen from any road or any house? A.—Yes, sir.

Mr. Waller—Trees about it? A.—Yes; trees and alders.

Mr. Waller—Place where a private meeting could be had?

Witness—I should judge so.

Mr. Waller—Did you ever meet Mary there? A.—No, sir.

Mr. Waller—Wouldn't your cow, in its innocence (laughter), sometimes wander up to the spring and you go after it when time for it to go home? A.—I know this—

Mr. Waller—Answer my question. Did your cow get there and you go after it? A.—Yes, sir.

Mr. Waller—It didn't come at call? A.—No, sir.

Mr. Waller—Never met Mary while up there with your cow?

Witness—No, sir; I never did.

Mr. Waller—Now, sir, did you know what the physical condition of Mary Stannard was, from her or your wife? A.—No, sir.

Mr. Waller—Do you know Rev. Mr. Eldridge? A.- Yes, sir.

Mr. Waller—Of Middletown?

Witness—Of Middletown? No, sir; the man I know is of Middlefield.

Mr. Waller—A part of the town?

Witness—That I don't know, Mr. Waller.

Mr. Waller—Now, sir, did you have any talk with Mr. Eldridge about this case? A.—Yes, sir.

Mr. Waller—Didn't you say to him substantially that it was folly to charge you with having intercourse with Mary Stannard, as about that time, or since, you knew from your wife that Mary Stannard had irregular menstruation? Or that it was folly to suppose that you knew the girl was in the family way, because your wife had told you she was regular in her periods? A.—No, sir.

Mr. Waller—Have any talk with him about this?

Witness—No, sir; I don't think we ever had any talk about Mary's physical condition.

Mr. Waller—Did you, before you went to the coroner's jury, Wednesday afternoon, know that it was claimed Mary Stannard was pregnant? A.—No, sir; don't think I did.

Mr. Waller—Or that she thought she was?

Witness—No, sir; don't think I ever heard a word on the subject.

Mr. Waller—Do you know Walter Green? A.—I do.

Mr. Waller—Did you have any talk on that Wednesday before you went to the coroner's jury?

· Witness—Don't recollect that I met Mr. Green.

Mr. Waller—Didn't say that Mary had got herself into trouble and was pregnant, and had laid it on to you?

· Witness—No, sir. I told you, Mr. Waller, that I didn't recollect that I met Mr. Green that day.

Mr. Waller—Did you say to Green that in fact she had got into pregnancy while at Guilford and committed suicide in consequence?

Witness—No, sir.

Mr. Waller—Mr. Hayden, you have told us Wednesday night you had a pleasant conversation with Luzerne Stevens about potatoes? A.—Yes, sir.

Mr. Waller—And that his child was in the house, and that Rachel Stevens also acted as midwife?

Mr. Waller—Then you were on pleasant terms with your neighbors? A.—I knew nothing to the contrary.

Mr. Waller—Now, sir, do you know if a person could have been seen going from your house into the barn door facing the street from Luzerne Stevens's window?

Witness—I have an impression that two cherry trees in my garden and a bush hid or obstructed the view.

Mr. Waller—Did you see that Wednesday afternoon anybody at the window while Mary Stannard was at your house?

Witness—No, sir. They may have been there. At any rate I did not see them.

Mr. Waller—You were quite intimate with the Stannards? I mean proper intimacy.

Witness—Yes, sir. Mary worked for my wife and the father for me.

Mr. Waller—Where did you get that Peruvian dollar?

Witness—I can't say. I think I got it up at the Vineyard.

Mr. Waller—How soon did you get money after you went to Middletown with Mary Stannard?

Witness—I got money on the 18th.

Mr. Waller—So you can't tell us where you got that dollar.

Witness—No, sir.

Mr. Waller—Now, when with Mary in Middletown, that was after you had talked with the stewards about arsenic being good to kill rats with? A.—Yes, sir.

Mr. Waller—You would have bought arsenic then if you had had money?

Witness—I think not. I had not fully made up my mind to buy.

Mr. Waller—Your intimacy with Mary was such that you couldn't ask her to loan you enough to buy the arsenic?

Witness—No, sir. I'll tell you why. I wanted to feed my horse. I told my wife I did not want to ask her (Mary) for the money.

Mr. Waller—Mr. Hayden, who was the first person, and when was it, you told you had bought arsenic?

Witness—I think it was Thursday morning, and the person my wife.

Mr. Waller—Did you tell your wife the questions the jury asked you?

Witness—I don't think I did. I know I did not Wednesday.

Mr. Waller—You knew pretty well then that you were an object of suspicion?

Witness—Yes; but not fully then.

Mr. Waller—Now, do you mean to tell us that you did not tell your wife about it that night?

Witness—I do; just that.

Mr. Waller—Sleep that night? A.—I did.

Mr. Waller—With your wife? A.—I did.

Mr. Waller—Did you act strange?

Witness—No, sir; I tried to act as naturally as possible.

Mr. Waller—Self-possessed and charged with murder, and you looked at her and she at you, and you had that power of self-possession that she did not discover anything?

Witness—I can't say that. I tried to act as naturally as possible.

Mr. Waller—Ate an ordinary breakfast next morning?

Witness—I don't remember. I know what we had been living on for some time—pork and potatoes.

Mr. Waller—When did you tell your wife?

Witness—Thursday forenoon.

Mr. Waller—Who was there?

Witness—Mrs. Davis was there, helping wife.

Mr. Waller—Now, sir, when suspicion pointed to you, did you tell her at that time that you had been to Middletown the day you went away, and bought arsenic that day; that you had taken the arsenic and thrown away the paper?

Witness—Not that I had thrown away the paper.

Mr. Waller—I did not ask that.

Witness to Mr. Waller—I told her that day that I bought arsenic on Tuesday.

Mr. Waller—What did your wife say to you about it?

Witness—Oh! Mr. Waller, I cannot remember. She was all broken up. [Mr. Jones remonstrated.]

Mr. Waller—Did she recover after the shock produced?

Witness—I think the next time she spoke about it was Sunday. I was taken away Friday morning.

Mr. Waller—Did you stay with your wife until you was taken away Friday? A.—I did not.

Mr. Waller—Where were you Friday?

Witness—I went to the funeral.

Mr. Waller—Did you stay with her that night before the arrest?

Witness—I was home, up stairs. Mrs. Davis stayed with wife below.

Mr. Waller—Did she mention to you anything about purchasing arsenic Friday or Thursday night? A.—I think not.

Mr. Waller (impressively)—Did she forget that her husband told her he had purchased arsenic?

Witness—I don't think it strange. I only wonder the poor woman is living to-day.

Mr. Waller—Yes! Who did you tell next?

Witness—William Minor and Alexander Johnson.

Mr. Waller—You were under arrest? A.—Yes.

Mr. Waller—Under Sheriff Hull's charge?

Witness—Under some sheriff. Yes; it was under Sheriff Hull's charge.

Mr. Waller—And to those brethren stewards on Friday; you told them! Who was present in the probate.office when you took them into the ante-room?

Witness—I don't know. There was a large crowd outside.

Mr. Waller—Was Judge Landon? Was Sheriff Hull?

Witness—Yes, sir.

Mr. Waller—Was Sheriff Hull where he could keep sight of you?

Witness—Sheriff Hull gave me permission to see them.

Mr. Waller—He did! Now, sir, did not just such a thing as you had told us occur in the probate office the next Monday?

Witness—I was not in there the next Monday. The court had adjourned to Coe's Hall.

Mr. Waller—I will not trouble you any further about that then. Did you tell anybody but your wife anything about your purchasing poison (arsenic) until you knew that it was to be published in a newspaper, if it had not been already, that you had been seen in Middletown and purchased some sort of abortion medicine?

Witness—I heard nothing of the sort.

Mr. Waller—How soon did you see a paper containing an account of the homicide?

Witness—I don't think I have ever seen an account in any paper.

Mr. Waller—Did you know that the body of Mary Stannard was to be exhumed? A.—I did.

Mr. Waller—From whom ?

Witness—At the table of my keeper, on Monday noon, the first day of my trial.

Mr. Waller—Now, sir, did you not know you were traced to the Tyler drug store ?

Witness—No, sir. That was not in the paper. Mr. Tyler said, months afterward, that he never would have thought of it again.

Mr. Waller—He did !

Witness—Yes, sir ; he said he never would unless he had seen my testimony.

Mr. Waller—Now, sir, Mr. Hayden, did you not see that paper before Sunday ?

Witness—I have never seen it, sir.

Mr. Waller—Very well. I won't trouble you to show it to you now. It is. the Middletown Sentinel. [Of what date ? Mr. Jones asked.]

Mr. Waller—Did you know Susan Hawley ? A.—I did.

Mr. Waller—Was there a pleasant intimacy, proper of course, between you ?

Witness—We were on good terms.

Mr. Waller—Did she not loan you that summer $75 ?

Witness—No, sir.

Mr. Waller—Did she never loan you $75 ?

Witness—Yes, sir ; that was in 1877.

Mr. Waller—I don't find fault with the time of paying it, as you paid interest on it. So Susan was on good terms with you ; did any hostility arise until the time of the homicide ?

Witness—Certainly not on my part. I never saw Susan much anyhow.

Mr. Waller—If you wanted to borrow, would it have been any trouble to borrow it of Susan ?

Witness (laugh)—I don't know, sir.

Mr. Waller—Mr. Hayden, when last did you see Mary Stannard alive ?

Witness—Shortly after 11 o'clock, Tuesday, September 3.

Mr. Waller—When you last saw her did she look depressed ?

Witness—I don't recollect, Mr. Waller.

Mr. Waller—Mr. Hayden, have you ever used arsenic yourself before 1878 ?

Witness—No, sir ; I never did.

Mr. Waller—Had you ever seen arsenic before that time to recognize it as arsenic ?

Witness—Not that I recollect.

Mr. Waller—Were you familiar with the operation of arsenic as a poison ?

Witness—No, sir ; I was not. I simply knew that it was a deadly poison.

Mr. Waller—Whether it would produce sleep or irritation or burning, or were you not acquainted at all with it ?

Witness—I was not.

Mr. Waller—Did you get in Middletown on that visit (September 3) anything except fullers' earth and arsenic ?

Witness—I did not.

Mr. Waller—If you were not familiar with arsenic or its opera- tion, and only knew it was a deadly poison, did you know September 3, 1878, how much it would take to kill ?

Witness—I knew it was a deadly poison, and that a very small amount would cause death.

Mr. Waller—How much ?

Witness—I know that enough taken on the point of a knife would cause death.

Mr. Waller—You knew it then ?

Witness—I supposed so.

Mr. Waller—How did you learn that a very little will produce death ? A.—I cannot say, sir.

Mr. Waller—You have said where you got the given knife. Now, where did you get the first one ?

Witness—I bought it of Monroe Burr in the winter of 1876 or 1877.

Mr. Waller—Can you tell where you bought the one previous to the Burr knife ?

Witness—I think wife gave it to me as a present.

Mr. Waller—Was the knife you used in your business the Burr knife ? A.—It was.

Mr. Waller—Was it near the size of what is called the Hayden knife ?

Witness—I think it was : am not sure. I think it was a small, two-bladed knife.

Mr. Waller—Did you ever have a knife two-bladed and about the size of the Hayden knife ? A.—I never did.

A pause ensued.

Mr. Waller—You told us when you reached Stannard's that Stevens was outdoors ? A.—I did not say that.

Mr. Waller—Well, where was he when you first saw him ?

Witness—Outdoors.

Mr. Waller—Now, before the coroner's jury you said you first saw Ben Stevens inside the house sitting down in the sitting-room ?

Witness—I was not questioned on the subject.

Mr. Waller said again—Did you say so ?

Witness—I was not questioned on that, and therefore I did not say so.

Mr. Waller—Answer my question : Will you swear that you did not say so ?

Witness—I'll swear that I don't remember saying so.

Mr. Waller—What time did you say you left the oyster supper in March ?

Witness—I was not questioned on that.

Mr. Waller—Well, I'll ask you now.

Witness—It was in the neighborhood of 9 o'clock.

Mr. Waller—And you were absent how long ?

Witness—Not exceeding ten minutes.

Mr. Waller here rested with the prisoner.

MR. HAYDEN'S TESTIMONY CLOSED.

The Re-Direct Examination and further Cross Inquiries.

Mr. Jones to Mr. Hayden—You say you purchased a knife of Monroe Burr, the knife before you. How much did you pay for it ?

Witness—Yes, sir, and paid fifty cents.

Mr. Jones—Where is it ?

Witness—The handle, when I was arrested, was in my tool chest, and if Mr. Hull did not take it from there, it is there now.

Mr. Jones—There was where you last saw it ?

Witness—Yes, sir. It was not black handled ; it was brown. I think it is at South Madison, locked up, if not taken away. The other knife I had not seen for years. Except those three knives and the one I bought the boy, I owned no other in Rockland. The knife my wife gave me was white handled, with a blade at each end.

Mr. Jones—You say you left the oyster supper at 9 o'clock ?

Witness—Yes, sir.

Mr. Jones—And went where ?

Witness—Went home to put the children to bed.

Mr. Jones—What was your custom about that ?

Witness—Always when at home I put the children to bed.

Mr. Jones—The oyster supper ; by whom was it gotten up and for what purpose ?

Witness—It was gotten up by the Ladies' Aid Society of the church at Rockland to liquidate the debt of $100 on the church. We had had one oyster supper in January and liquidated one-half of that hundred.

Mr. Jones—When you went to put the children to bed did any one go with you ? A.—No ; there did not.

Mr. Jones—What was your business at the supper?

Witness—To take the name of every person who paid for supper, and in some cases to take fares. We were giving away bed-quilts, and every one who paid for a supper had a chance on these quilts.

Mr. Jones—When you were absent who took the names?

Witness—I took the names of all before I went. Wife and I sat at the table with those who ate at the first spread. When the second table was set I was back and took the names. The first table had been completed and I then went to put the children to bed. That guides me in my recollection. There was an interim of a half to three-quarters of an hour before the second table was ready. While the second table was being prepared I went to the children. I have no distinct recollection of the exact time, but I was gone from the church but a few moments.

Mr. Jones—The question was asked if you had borrowed money of Susan Hawley?

Witness—It was in the spring of 1877. I had a note which had become due, and wife informed me that Mary Stannard had said that Susan had some money.

Mr. Jones—Was it your note?

Witness—The note was drawn by my wife and signed by wife and myself.

Mr. Jones—Mr. Hayden, the question has been asked how many times you were ever at the Stannard house. State how many times you were there while in Rockland.

Witness—I don't remember but four times. One was when I went to see about the money wife had informed me of ; and once to get cucumbers. The Stannard boy had asked me to come, and once on the night of September 3 ; and once after some apples. That is all I remember, Mr. Jones.

Mr. Jones—You were not in the habit of going there?

Witness—No, sir.

Mr. Jones—The question was asked you the other day about a knife like that you used to peel apples or pears with being used in other families?

Witness—I don't recollect that question about other families.

Mr. Jones—Which would be most convenient to peel pears with, a broad or narrow-bladed knife?

Witness—I should prefer a narrow-bladed.

Mr. Jones—Mr. Hayden, when you returned from South Madison Monday, you had been absent how long?

Witness—I went away Sunday morning at 9 o'clock.

Mr. Jones—Had you any knowledge that people had gone abroad to work on their farms Monday morning?

Mr. Jones—Had you any knowledge on Tuesday afternoon whether any of your neighbors, except those you had seen, were away? A.—I had not.

Mr. Jones—Did you know where Luzerne Stevens was?

·Witness—I did not.

Mr. Jones—Or where the ladies were? A.—I did not.

Mr. Jones—Hadn't been around to see? A.—No, sir.

Mr. Jones—Is there shrubbery near the Ribbon Path?

Witness—There is.

Mr. Jones—Don't you think if you were crossing the path on a murderous mission you wouldn't have shut your eyes and not noticed whether any one was coming down the road?

Mr. Waller thought it an improper question.

Mr. Jones passed it.

Mr. Jones—The question was asked you why you didn't buy your oats in South Madison Monday; what was your answer?

Witness—My answer was that I had no store account; that I didn't think I could get trusted at Myron Hull's store because a former minister at Rockland had run in debt $150. Mr. Hull had sued the church, supposing the church was personally responsible, and was defeated, and then he swore never to trust another Methodist minister. (Laughter.)

Mr. Jones—Did you ever buy a bag of oats at South Madison to take to Rockland?

Witness—No, sir; there are fourteen hills to climb. (Laughter.)

Mr. Jones—Rather lively hills?

Witness—Yes; Rather hard to climb.

Mr. Jones—You spoke of getting a bag of oats in Durham on that Tuesday; was it a long bag?

Witness—No, sir; it was a broad bag. I don't know the distinction, Mr. Jones, between a bag and a sack. I know they now come one hundred pounds. I did not speak of it as a bag, but as a bushel.

MARY E. STANNARD'S ROCKLAND HOME.

Mr. Jones—Mr. Hayden, a good deal has been said about that horse of yours. Which is the oldest, you or the horse?

Witness—The horse I think is about seventeen years old. (Laughter.)

Mr. Jones—Did you not think it dangerous to leave the reins in charge of one of your children?

Witness—The horse was very gentle, Mr. Jones; I had no fears.

Mr. Jones—We'll pass to that spot near the spring, where you got out to get a drink of water. You got out there and passed the reins to your little boy?

Witness—I stood close to the vehicle. I did not consider it a dangerous operation.

Mr. Jones—When you stopped at Stannard's, how then?

Witness—Mr. Stannard came out, and as I turned to speak to him I saw Mary and Ben Stevens.

Mr. Jones—Mr. Hayden, I want to call your attention to the road up by Stannard's (going to map). You say you never heard of Big Rock or Fox Ledge Rock or Whippoorwill Rock?

Witness—I did not say that.

Mr. Watrous—You misquoted him. He said he never had been there.

Witness—I said at the trial at South Madison that I never had heard of either of them.

Mr. Jones—Now, Mr. Hayden, had you known of paths across? Did you know of a path opposite the Stannard house leading to the cart-path?

Witness—I did not. I observed a path leading to the woods. I did not know where it led to. I saw the path from the road, but had no knowledge of the foot-path.

Mr. Jones—Where had you purchased, while living in Rockland, your Paris green?

Witness—At Tyler's; I purchased it for the potatoes in 1877 and 1878. I think I made but one purchase in each year.

Mr. Jones—Why not purchase it at Meigs's in South Madison?

Witness—I don't know. I don't know whether he kept it. I never was in his store enough to get acquainted with his store.

Mr. Jones—Why not in Durham?

Witness—I cannot give any reason except that when I wanted anything in the apothecary's line I went to Middletown for it.

Mr. Jones—How many druggists do you know by sight in Middletown?

Witness—I know Woodward and Tyler. I once went into the store of one other and bought a cigar. It was on—it was on Main street ; I think next door to the free reading-room, west side of Main street. I had no acquaintance with the others.

Mr. Jones—Mr. Hayden, were your children in the habit of going into the cellar? A.—They seldom went in.

Mr. Jones—Why?

Witness—They said they were afraid of rats. (Laughter.) I went with them once.

Mr. Jones—You were asked if you were ever with Mary Stannard in any lot or out-of-the-way place ; what was your answer?

Witness—I never was.

Mr. Jones—Did you ever make her any presents?

Witness—No, sir. I once bought her a pair of shoes, but it was out of her wages.

Mr. Jones—Who was with you when you bought that pair of shoes?

Witness—My wife. We bought them at Durham, at Leach's. Mary wanted the shoes, and we said we would get them. I never inquired for fullers' earth at Durham and South Madison, and owing to an experience I had in Hartford. I went to several druggists there, and finally had to go to a wholesale druggist. I don't know of any families that use it in Rockland except my own. I had knowledge of fullers' earth from my wife. I did, I think, one term have a room in the college building at Middletown. I don't know whether the Industrial School building is to be seen from the building. If it is, it could not from the windows of that room. I could have concealed the tools on my return home from Middletown if I had intended to hide my visit from her. [Mr. Waller objected ; was the witness an expert in hiding tools?]

Mr. Jones—You remember you asked a quiet little question, Mr. Waller.

Witness—Yes ; my examination at the jury of inquest was very short. I was asked nothing about my purchase of molasses or fullers' earth ; or whether I went to my wood lot.

Mr. Jones—You saw Dr. Bailey at Middletown after your purchase there. Will you state what was said?

Witness—Dr. Bailey first spoke and said good morning, Mr. Hayden. I said good morning, doctor. We met at the corner of Court and Main streets as I came out of Tyler's drug store. He asked me if I was still living in Rockland. He asked me how my family was. I told him very well. Wife was getting along as well as could be expected, as wife had just had a child, about three weeks before. He asked me if she was troubled. I can't give you the exact words.

Mr. Jones—Well, never mind; give us the substance.

Witness—He asked me if she was troubled the same way as in her former pregnancy, and I said no, and asked him if he had many such cases. It would be hard for me to state it, but Doctor—

Mr. Jones—Was it about irregularity of menstruation?

Witness—Yes. In the first place she was troubled with ulceration of the vagina.

Mr. Jones—Now you may go on.

Witness—I asked him if he had many such cases. I asked him how his family was. I asked him of the whereabouts of a young lady I had formerly known. That was all.

Mr. Jones—That was all, and he introduced the conversation?

Witness—Yes, sir. About Mr. Green, as you ask, I went for Dr. Bailey to have him visit Mr. Green, a sick man in our place.

Mr. Jones—Mr. Hayden, are you left-handed or right-handed?

Witness—Right-handed.

Mr. Jones—Use your left or right in whittling?

Witness—Always with my right.

Mr. Jones to Mr. Hayden—That's all.

THE STATE INQUIRES AGAIN.

Mr. Waller—That horse, you say, was about seventeen years old and a gentle one? A.—It was.

Mr. Waller—You had no fear from so aged a horse that it would run away or cut up uncomfortable capers?

Witness—I had no fear of its running away.

Mr. Waller—But were afraid of its cutting up capers?

Witness—I was.

Mr. Waller—When he panted, it was not because he was nervous that made the carriage shake, but the panting? A.—Yes.

Mr. Waller—Then he was panting when Mary was with you at the spring, not excited ? A.—No, sir.

Mr. Waller—At Stannard's the horse rested how long ?

Witness—Not over five minutes.

Mr. Waller—Did you drive that horse from Durham carefully and gently ?

Witness—I think I can answer that yes.

Mr. Waller—Well, sir, is that your answer ? A.—Yes.

Mr. Waller—Did you stop between Middletown and Durham to give the horse a rest ? A.—I did.

Mr. Waller—And at Stannard's the horse stopped about five minutes ?

Witness—Yes, about five minutes.

Mr. Waller—After that rest you drove carefully down the hill, and slowly ?

Witness—I think he went his usual gait as when I was behind him.

Mr. Waller—Mr. Hayden, your habit was, if I remember, when going to Middletown, to go one road and come back another ?

Witness—I said sometimes I went one way and came back the other.

Mr. Waller—How often were you in the habit of driving or walking past the Stannard house, say in the summer season ?

Witness—I can't answer it. Well, what do you mean, Mr. Waller ?

Mr. Waller—Well, I'll make it plain. How many times from May, 1878, to September 3, 1878, were you up that road as far as the Stannard house ?

Witness asked—Any farther ?

Mr. Waller—No, sir ; stop there. Well, up as far as the Stannard house or farther ?

Witness—I can't answer that question.

Mr. Waller—Do you think fifty times ? A.—No, sir.

Mr. Waller—Do you think thirty times ?

Witness—I said I couldn't tell. I don't know.

Mr. Waller—Twenty times ? A.—I can't say.

Mr. Waller—Sure as many as ten times ?

Witness—I can't say ; no recollection.

Mr. Waller—Sure of once, September 3 ?

Witness—Yes, sir ; and August 9, when the tornado—

Mr. Waller—Answer my question ; how many times? You are sure of twice?

Witness—Yes ; I am sure of those times.

Mr. Waller—When going after your cow, did you ever go up as far as here (twenty rods below the spring) where my pointer is ?

Witness—I don't know, sir.

Mr. Waller—Did you tell Mr. Jones there was a path leading into the road here pointing on map ?

Witness—I told him I didn't know there was a path by the Stannard house.

Mr. Waller—Back of the path was the foliage dense in 1878; ten or fifteen feet back ?

Witness—I can answer both yes and no.

Mr. Waller—Was it so dense that a person could step back and not be seen ?

Witness—Yes, sir ; in the place where you put the pointer. A portion of the way in the path one would be concealed. [Witness rose up and pointed on map, speaking quietly and pleasantly.]

Mr. Waller—Now be seated, Mr. Hayden, if you desire to. Did you never before, if not on that day, see this path ?

Witness—I did not.

Mr. Waller—A Methodist minister had cheated the storekeeper ?

Witness—I did not say that.

Mr. Waller—He hadn't paid ?

Witness—No, the society had not paid.

Mr. Waller—How long did you know Henry Woodward ?

Witness—I knew him only by sight. I don't think I spoke to the man over once in my life.

Mr. Waller—Did you not say at the hearing in Madison that you did not know whether Tyler knew your name and occupation or not ?

Witness—I said I did not, but supposed he did.

Mr. Waller—Did Dr. Matthewson doctor in your family in 1876, 1877, 1878? A.—Yes, sir.

Mr. Waller—Did you not buy of him a breast pump ?

Witness—I borrowed it.

Mr. Waller—Did you not know then that he kept arsenic for sale and had for years ? A.—I did not.

Mr. Waller—Did you not know that he kept drugs?

Witness—Not for sale. I always knew that doctors had their medicines.

Mr. Waller—Did you ever buy of Matthewson?

Witness—I don't know that I ever did.

Mr. Waller—Didn't you expect him to attend your wife in confinement? A.—I did not.

Mr. Waller—When did you commence to learn the carpenter's trade, Mr. Hayden?

Witness—I think when I was sixteen years old.

Mr. Waller—Any before that did your occupation lead to the knowledge of slaughtering domestic animals?

Witness—I think I can say yes or no to that.

Mr. Waller—Did your father for awhile carry on the occupation of a butcher?

Witness—Part of the time when I was living in Somerset.

Mr. Waller—Did you not for a time drive a butcher cart in Somerset? A.—I did. It was father's market.

Mr. Waller—And how long were you keeping market?

Witness—I should say it was a year. It might exceed that.

Mr. Waller—Did you ever see him or assist him butcher animals?

Witness—I did.

Mr. Waller—Was it a boyish recreation of yours to see him butcher animals? A.—I can't say that.

Mr. Waller—Did you ever assist in it? A.—I don't think I did.

Mr. Waller—Ever butcher little lambs?

Mr. Jones—Well! what's the object of all this? Suppose a man has killed a calf in his early life, it don't show who killed that girl.

Mr. Waller—It's very greatly to his credit. That's all.

MR. JONES CLOSES.

Mr. Jones—How old were you, Mr. Hayden, when your father kept that market?

Witness—About twelve years old. Father lived four miles from the market.

Mr. Jones—Well! twelve years old; that was fifteen years ago? A.—Seventeen years; I am nearly thirty.

Mr. Jones—That's all, Mr. Hayden.

MRS. HAYDEN.

[From a photograph taken December, 1879.]

MRS. HAYDEN'S TESTIMONY.

The testimony of Mrs. Hayden was a complete corroboration of that given by her husband. She testified that his knife (the one assumed by the state to have been the weapon used at the time of the tragedy) was not out of the house the afternoon of the murder ; that her little boy had it, and that Mr. Hayden and the boy had cut themselves on a former occasion in using this knife. Mr. Hayden, by direction, showed to the jury the scars of a cut on one of his fingers, made, the witness testified to her knowledge, with the knife.

As to occurrences at about the time of the murder—the day previous and on the day of the tragedy—Mrs. Hayden testified on the direct examination :

Mr. Jones—When did your husband go to Madison last before the murder ?

Witness—He went on Sunday morning about 9 o'clock and returned on Monday afternoon about half-past 3.

Mr. Jones—What time did Mary come to your house on Monday ?

Witness—It was about 9 o'clock.

Mr. Jones—Did you have conversation with Mary ?

Witness—I did.

Mr. Jones—What did she say she came for ?

Witness—When she came in she said she had waited as long as she could without seeing me. Said she thought I would want to see her by that time. She came home unexpectedly from Guilford. She told me before she went that she expected to stay some length of time if Willie got along well at Mrs. Studley's. She said she hoped he would get along well.

Mr. Jones—Did she tell you why she came back from Guilford ?

Witness—She said that Willie was troublesome at Mr. Studley's, and she had come home hoping that she could make arrangements to leave him at home. She said if she could make such an arrangement, they would pay her more at Studley's. This was the substance of her conversation.

Mr. Jones—How long did she remain at your house that morning?

Witness—She remained a short time. While there she went to the well and got me a pail of water.

Mr. Jones—Where did you next see Mary?

Witness—I saw her the same day, going down past my house, with a pail in her hand.

Mr. Jones—When did you next see her?

Witness—It was a short time; I should think about twenty minutes. She returned and came into the house. She seemed annoyed. Said she had been to Enos Stevens's after butter, and did not find him at home. She rested a few minutes and then went out of the door. She had her pail with her. I don't remember whether I saw her going up the road toward home.

Mr. Jones—When did you next see Mary?

Witness—I should think it was about 4 o'clock in the afternoon on the same day. She came into the south door of our house.

Mr. Jones—For what purpose did she say she came at that time?

Witness—She said she came to borrow a rake for her father.

Mr. Jones—Where was your husband at that time?

Witness—He sat at the east dining-room window smoking.

Mr. Jones—What were you doing when Mary came in?

Witness—I was in the dining-room tending baby.

Mr. Jones—What did Mary say to your husband?

Witness—She said: "How do you do, Mr. Hayden." He replied, "How do you do." She told him that her father wanted to borrow a rake, and he started to go towards the barn to get it.

Mr. Jones—Did Mary go with him? A.—She did not.

Mr. Jones—What was Mary doing while your husband had gone to the barn?

Witness—She was tending my baby. She took my baby out of my arms as soon as she came in.

Mr. Jones—When did you next see your husband?

Witness—I saw him coming from the barn with the rake. Mary

asked me to take the baby, and I told her to put it in the cradle. She did so, and she and I then moved toward the open door.

Mr. Jones—When you reached the door where was Mr. Hayden?

Witness—He stood in the yard in front of the veranda with the rake in his hand.

Mr. Jones—What took place next?

Witness—Mary stepped on to the veranda, and, I think, on to the ground. We all stood near together. I heard her ask him if he was in a hurry for the rake, and he said no ; she could keep it as long as she wished. Mr. Hayden and I then went back into the house, and Mary, as I supposed, started for home.

Mr. Jones—That, as I understand you, was the first time your husband saw Mary after his return from Madison? A.—Yes, sir.

Mr. Jones—What did Mr. Hayden do after Mary started for home with the rake?

Witness—He sat down by the same window and continued his smoking. He was there some time, chatting and smoking. I should think he was there three-quarters of an hour.

Mr. Jones—Where were your two older children when Mary was at your house at this time?

Witness—I think they were around the house, but I cannot tell where. Think they may have been over to Mr. Luzerne Stevens's.

Mr. Jones—I want to ask you again if Mary went out to the barn on Monday, or went out with Mr. Hayden?

Witness—She did not go out of the house until she started for home.

Mr. Jones—When did you next see Mary?

Witness—I think it was the next morning about 9 o'clock. She came into the kitchen door, and said her father wanted to borrow a pitchfork. I told her she could have it, but would have to get it herself, as I had not at that time been out of the house since my baby was born. She started for the barn, and soon after I heard her call: " Mrs. Hayden." I went to the door and she had a fork in her hand. The center tine was broken out, and she asked me if there was any other. I told her I did not know. She said she guessed that would do. She then came up to the door, and, without coming in, talked a moment and then went away.

Mr. Jones—Mrs. Hayden, was Mary at your barn on Monday or

Tuesday, except at the time you have stated, and was there any one with her when she went to the barn?

Witness—She was not, and there was no one with her to the best of my knowledge.

Mr. Jones—When did you next see her?

Witness—It was between 9:30 and 10 o'clock on the same day, when she came from the store. She came in and stayed about half an hour. She was in the habit of coming to my house, and was always welcome. I should have stated before that I think the children went with her to the store.

Mr. Jones—Did you have conversation with Mary on other subjects? I mean religious subjects?

Witness—Yes, sir. I often talked with her on religious subjects, and she showed an interest in religious matters.

Mr. Jones—State who went with her the last (Tuesday) morning when she went away.

Witness—My two children went with her, up to her house.

Mr. Jones—What did Mary say about returning with the children?

Witness—She said she would come in sight of the house with them. This was her custom when they went to her house. I desired that she should do this, so that I could see them when she left them. She would come down below the spring with them, just above the fork of the road.

Mr. Jones—What time were the children to come home that day?

Witness—They were to stay an hour, I believe: this was their usual time of staying.

Mr. Jones—State if, in about an hour, you were on the lookout for the children?

Witness—I was. I sat at the north dining-room window. I first saw a carriage up toward Stannard's house, above the spring. While I was looking I thought I saw the top of a carriage come to a stand still. I thought it might be Mr. Hayden and that he had stopped for the children. The carriage stopped but a minute or two, and then came on. I first saw them plainly just above the fork of the road.

Mr. Jones—Did your husband go away on Tuesday, and if so, at what time?

Witness—He did. He went away Tuesday morning about half-past 6 o'clock. We were out of feed at that time. I told him if he was going I wanted him to get me some sugar, molasses and fullers' earth.

Mr. Jones—Did Mr. Hayden tell you where he was going on Tuesday?

Witness—He did not. Sometimes he told me where he was going and sometimes he did not. He usually bought his feed in Durham.

Mr. Jones—Have you any personal knowledge about an arrangement Mr. Hayden had with a party in Middletown about buying agricultural tools?

Witness—In the summer of 1877 I heard a conversation between Mr. Burton, of Middletown, and Mr. Hayden about a wagon Mr. Hayden was going to buy of Burton and pay for it in produce. He afterward bought a wagon elsewhere ; and, while I was with him, went to Mr. Burton's and told him that, as he had got a wagon, he would take his pay in carpenter's tools.

Mr. Jones—What time did your husband return on Tuesday?

Witness—About quarter past 12.

Mr. Jones—What did he bring with him?

Witness—He brought some feed, molasses, sugar and a box of fullers' earth.

Mr. Jones—Will you tell us just here whether you were troubled with rats or not?

Witness—We were very much troubled. There were rat-holes in the chambers when we moved there. There were so many in the cellar that we could not keep anything there without covering it with something that the rats could not gnaw through.

Mr. Jones—Had you had any conversation with your husband about getting arsenic?

Witness—I had, and I told him that I was afraid to have it in the house. I told him to get "ratsbane." I did not know that arsenic and ratsbane were the same thing until I heard Professor Johnson say they were the same, in court.

Mr. Jones—When did Mr. Hayden first tell you that he had purchased arsenic?

Witness—It was the Sunday after the homicide and while I was in South Madison. I don't remember that anybody else was present.

Mr. Jones—You may state how the conversation about arsenic came up.

Witness—On the Sunday before I saw something in the paper about his going to Middletown. I asked him on Sunday if he got the things in Middletown. He said that he got the sugar, molasses and oats at Durham, and the fullers' earth and arsenic in Middletown.

Mr. Jones—After your husband's return what did he do? Tell in your own way what he did up to tea time.

Witness—After he came home he brought the things into the house, putting the bag into the store-room, and carried the other things into the pantry. He then went out, and I thought around the barn. He then came in, asked what I was going to have for dinner, built a fire in the kitchen stove, went down cellar and got the oysters and took them out under the fir tree and opened them.

Mr. Jones—Was anybody at your house at the time?

Witness—I don't remember that there was.

Mr. Jones—What did he open the oysters with?

Witness—A pocket-knife.

Mr. Jones (handing the witness a knife)—Is that the knife?

Witness (after looking at the knife for some time)—It looks like the knife. My husband had but one knife, to the best of my knowledge. After he had opened the oysters he came in with the oysters and the knife in his hand. I took the oysters and knife, and, after wiping the knife, put it on the kitchen shelf. I told him I wanted it to peel some pears in the afternoon. Mr. Hayden then set the table for dinner, and in a short time I cooked the oysters. Mr. Hayden and the children sat down and ate dinner together, and I held the baby. After they got through I made toast for my dinner, and he held the baby while I ate. The dishes were not washed at that time. I being sick, Mr. Hayden did most of the work. He cleared off the table and put the things in the pantry. I think this was between a quarter and half-past 1. After this he did the chamber work, which consisted in making three beds. That noon he brought me a letter, which contained an administrator's account from my brother. This was sent for us to sign. It was the account of the settlement of my mother's estate. That paper was eventually returned to the administrator. The estate consisted principally of wood land, and had fallen in value. After

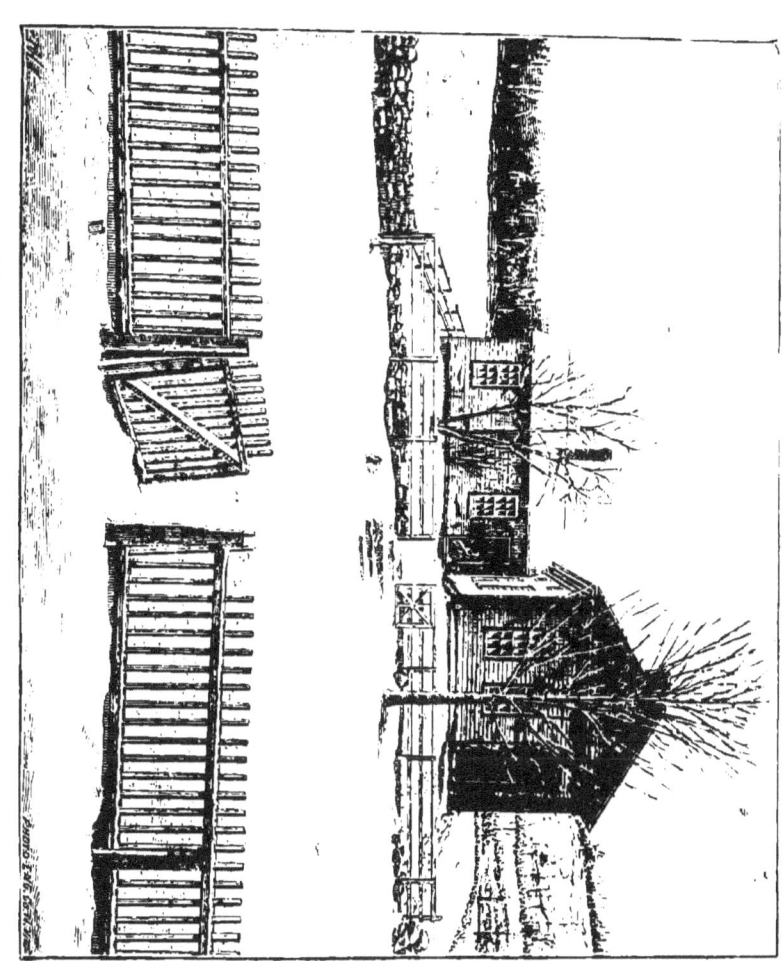

MR. STEVENS'S—OPPOSITE MR. HAYDEN'S.

[The point of observation from which the State claimed Mr. Hayden and Mary E. Stannard were seen going to the barn together the day before the murder.]

dinner we sat down to examine this account, and went over it, item by item. We were twenty or twenty-five minutes looking it over and signing it. After we had examined the account, Mr. Hayden laid down on the floor and played with the children ten or fifteen minutes. Then he said he was going over in the swamp to throw out some wood. We only had a few apple-tree twigs at home to burn at that time. He started for the wood lot, I think, about a quarter-past 2. I cannot say whether he went out of the kitchen or dining-room door. The children went out with him. I was sitting at my favorite window in the dining-room. I saw him going down the road toward Mr. Stevens's barn. I saw him as he was nearing the fork of the road. The understanding was that the children should go as far as the fork of the road and then return, and they did so. I next saw him getting over the bars at Burr's farm. Then I saw him a very short distance from the bars going toward the woods. When nearing Mr. Stevens's barn he threw a kiss to me. I know that my husband had a turnip patch, but I don't know exactly where it was, as I had never been to it. The next time I saw Mr. Hayden, after seeing him going toward the wood lot, was on the edge of the potato patch, near the house. I heard him call Emma, and I went to the window, when he told me to send him a basket to pick up some potatoes. I went into the kitchen to find Emma and I went to the window, when he told me to send him a basket, and just then he came to the back door and came in, and I did no more about it. I think I saw him take a basket from the sink room. I afterward saw him and Emma in the potato patch. I did not notice whether he was picking up potatoes or digging them after he went back into the patch. I think he brought the potatoes into the cellar, as I thought I heard him emptying them. Afterward I saw him and Emma picking up chips.

Mr. Jones—Did you say anything to him about going to the woods on that day?

Witness—I did. I tried to discourage him, as it was so warm. He said he must do it so that I would have some wood while he was away at work for Mr. Davis. I saw him on the way to the wood lot until my vision was obscured by the foliage on the trees in the swamp. That evening he helped me get tea. He also went into the parlor and wrote a postal card to Jason Dudley. It was in reference to a school. I don't think it was sent. The postal may be in Mr. Hayden's desk now, but I don't know. The postal card was not completed when he was informed of the death of Mary Stannard.

Mr. Jones here produced a bundle of clothing, and asked Mrs. Hayden to pick out the clothing that her husband wore on the day of the homicide.

Mr. Jones—Has that clothing ever been washed, to your knowledge? A.—No, sir.

Mr. Jones—When were you first informed of the death of Mary Stannard?

Witness—I think it was after six o'clock on Tuesday, when Jennie Stevens came in and told me about it. My husband was in the parlor at the time writing. He came out into the kitchen and went out doors. I heard him talking with some one outside. He returned about eight o'clock in the evening. As he came in he went into the sink-room and took down his coat and put it on. He said he was going with Charley Scranton for the coroner. I think he said he was going to Henry Stone's. I told him I could not stay alone, because I felt so badly and nervous. He went out and afterward came back, saying that he would not go. There was a wagon there at the time.

Mr. Jones—Mrs. Hayden, from the time you first knew Mary Stannard to the time of her death, was there anything like intimacy between Herbert H. Hayden and Mary Stannard? [Deep silence.]

Witness (solemnly)—None.

Mr. Jones—How often have they ever been in the same vehicle?

Witness—Three times. The first was in the summer of 1877. I had received an invitation from Mrs. Talcott Davis to go up there for cherries. Mary was working for me then. I invited her to go. We all went. We went and returned before dark. The second time was when she was sick, when she got her face and hands poisoned. I got some of my school boys to take her home on a hand sled. Mr. Hayden went up after her. It was after he had borrowed the horse to go to South Madison in the afternoon. Her father had said she was able to come up and do a little and help take care of the children.

Mr. Jones—You requested Mr. Hayden to go? A.—I did.

Mr. Jones—Now as to the third time?

Witness—It was when she went to Guilford, in 1878. After I

closed my school, in the last of February, Mr. Hayden had two
weeks more to teach in South Madison, and I wanted to go down
and visit, and we wanted the house, pigs and poultry taken care of ;
and I owed Mary a little money, and I told her that, if she would
come down and look after things a little, I would pay her when I
came back, and Mr. Hayden should take her to Middletown to get
some things I knew she wanted. I paid her $9 when I came home,
for they (Mr. Stannard's people) were hard pressed for money, and
wanted the money to use. So after she went to work at Guilford
she earned some money there, and, of course, had a chance to spend
it. She had dry goods she bought there. After that she was
working at Mrs. Studley's, and earned some money at gathering
whortleberries, and I told her I would keep my promise and have
Mr. Hayden take her to Middletown so she could spend her money.

Mr. Jones—Do you know what date that was?

Witness—The 14th or 15th of August. The baby was born
about that time ; I recollect it by that.

The cross-examination was short and was conducted by Mr.
Waller.

Mr. Waller—Mary was at your house just before the baby was
born a number of times? A.—Yes, sir.

Mr. Waller—Wasn't she at your house frequently after the baby
was born ?

Witness—She was a few times. The days she was whortleberrying she came in often ; when not specially busy she was at the
house perhaps on an average three times a week. She came to sew
on the machine sometimes.

Mr. Waller—On the Monday before the murder, I think you
said, she came in at 7 o'clock and said she could not wait any longer
without seeing you ? A.—Yes, sir.

Mr. Waller—Did you ask her why she did not walk down
Sunday afternoon when she knew you were all alone ?

Witness—I did not.

Mr. Waller—Do you know of any reason why she did not ?

Witness—No, sir.

Mr. Waller—When she came down that morning did you
remark to her that she looked nervous and distressed ?

Witness—Yes, sir.

Mr. Waller—Did you say, you don't look like yourself ?

Witness—I said, you don't look natural.

Mr. Waller—How did she usually act?

Witness—She was usually laughing and talking.

Mr. Waller—Did she not say she felt as if she would like to be dead?

Witness—She said she felt like swearing. She said she was a good mind to kill herself.

Mr. Waller—Did she tell you what the matter was?

Witness—She didn't then.

Mr. Waller—Did you understand it to refer to a little petty trouble with the child?

Witness—She had told me of something that had happened to her before she left a certain place. She told me privately.

Mr. Waller—Something you never told before?

Witness—Yes; I told it to Mrs. Gilbert Stone and Miss Davis.

Mr. Waller—Who else?

Witness—I don't remember. I think I told some others.

Mr. Waller—We will leave that topic for the present. Did it not occur to you that it was strange that Mary was at your house that morning? A.—No, sir.

Mr. Waller—I am asking your attention to the Tuesday morning of the day she died. Did your husband tell you he was going to Middletown? A.—I do not remember.

Mr. Waller—Don't you remember that he never said a word to you about going to Middletown?

Witness—Don't remember; think he did not say.

Mr. Waller—You were troubled with rats in that house, were you not?

Witness—I think I may safely say so.

Mr. Waller—Do you remember a time when you were not troubled?

Witness—It was about seven months that we were troubled.

Mr. Waller—How many times did you talk with Mr. Hayden about buying poison? A.—Several times.

Mr. Waller—When was it talked about?

[Witness broke down and cried. Checking her tears, she resumed.]—It was about the 10th of August. That was not the first time.

Mr. Waller—Never mind that.

Witness—He said he was going to.

Mr. Waller—You didn't know he had bought arsenic the day the girl died ; didn't know of it the day the girl died ; didn't know of it when he was arrested : you didn't know it till Sunday ? (Profound silence.)

Witness—I didn't know of it then. As I told you before, it is indistinct, but it seems to me that he said something about going to get it, but I could not swear to it.

Mr. Waller—If your husband had told you he bought arsenic, you would have remembered it, would you not ?

Witness—It seems as if he did, but I cannot be sure. There has been so much said that I do not recollect.

Mr. Waller—You testified nothing at Madison about it ?

Witness—There was nothing said about it. I testified to what I knew he bought.

Mr. Waller—Madam, was there anybody there on Tuesday, when your husband left your house, that saw him when you did and knows when he left the house ?

Witness—I know of none, nor of any that saw my husband crossing over by the Burr barn when I saw him. My boy saw the knife in the house when Mr. Hayden was gone. I know of nobody else that saw it. I did state in my opening testimony that the accused is my husband, that we have been married eight years, and that I have had three children by him. I stated that he always treated me well, and I do now continue to have affection for him and confidence in him, and that if he is punished it will be an unjust punishment inflicted upon him, for all that I know now.

[Profound silence. Wait a moment, Mr. Jones said.]

Mr. Waller—The question comes in now. It is the only question of the kind.

To Witness—Wait and give them time to object.

Mr. Waller—As the accused was your husband, the father of your children, and treated you well ; and as you believe, if he is punished, it will be unjust, is not your mind in such a condition that you would say something, even if not true, that would help him or save him ?

Both counsel for defence, quickly and with voices raised—Don't answer that question.

Mr. Waller (rising)—I would not say an unkind word to this

poor woman under any circumstances. Her devotion challenges the admiration and respect of all, and that she would exaggerate, prevaricate or commit perjury implies no censure upon her or upon womanhood. An opposite course may be possible in the higher life that Utopians think may be reached, but I can think that a wife who loves her husband as her life, that has full confidence in him, and knows that he is liable to an ignominious punishment—and a little faith is enough, if no bigger than a grain of mustard seed—and if she thinks he is liable to capital punishment, that a good woman, a true woman, could, by the natural operation of her mind, exaggerate, prevaricate, or commit a perjury to save him. I say nothing amiss of that poor woman that I could not say of my wife, dearly as I love her and the six children with whom God has blessed us. I say freely of my own wife that, if I thought she would hesitate to prevaricate, bold as the doctrine is, or even commit perjury to save me from a dreadful fate, I would not love her as much as I do now. It is a statement of fact I make, and a wife will always do that for her husband, until that perfect condition is reached which the Utopian dreams of. And my suggestion is not malignant, nor has it bad elements, but speaks only of the love and fidelity of that woman. An insult? Why, for centuries it was not allowed a woman to testify for her husband. The principle was that husband and wife are one, and even now in Connecticut the law is so that a wife cannot be compelled to go on the stand and testify against her husband. We couldn't, and we wouldn't if we could, for we wouldn't have a wife testify against her husband ; 'but the purport of the question is to fairly present the case to the triers.

Mr. Watrous—I am not surprised that the gentleman was not astonished that such a question should not arouse indignation. It is an insult to that lady, an insult from its very component parts. It asks if believing her husband innocent—a suggestion utterly incompatible with perjury being needful—that she could before God tell what is false for what is true. Seductively as the case has been presented, my learned friend knows his question is improper—improper legally ; but to ask if a witness upon the witness stand is ready to lie, with the word of God in her hands, is an affront. It is very ingenious to take this occasion—one improper as I say, but not censoriously—to ask if my witness would not lie under oath to save anybody. I respect the character of the wife as deeply as any can, even as my learned friend can. But it is wrong to ask this woman here—faithful, true, and an honor to her sex—before God and the heaven to which she is going, if she will tell a lie. In my practice as a lawyer I never knew such a question to be asked. We have no fear of the answer, but we ask that the witness be no more treated in that way, however good the motive may be. And the sweet things my friend has said about wifely faith should be saved for the time the arguments are made and not used certainly at this stage.

Mr. Waller—The question was to show the bias of the witness, and the extent.

The Court—We hardly think it a proper question to ask.

Mr. Waller to Mrs. Hayden—Madam, I have no further questions to ask.

Mr. Jones—Wait a moment, Mrs. Hayden. When Mary came home from the Studleys, do you know from any source what her physical condition was?

Witness—Not at that time. No direct knowledge.

Mr. Jones—Did you have a conversation with her on the subject, and when?

Witness—Think it was in the latter part of June or first of July. She said she was in a condition peculiar to females. She was washing at our house at the time. She spoke about feeling like swearing and killing herself. She came in as I was telling Mrs. Davis of a post-mortem examination performed on a relative of hers. She spoke that morning of having had trouble with her child. She spoke of it that morning, but had spoken particularly about it the morning before. In answer to a question from Mr. Waller as to my reasons for not inquiring, she said she had left a certain place which I will not name—

Mr. Jones—Did she say she left a particular place because of some attempted action by a party in that place?

(Objected to.)

[Mr. Jones said it ought to go to the jury that she felt like killing herself because of this trouble at that house. Mr. Watrous said what Mary said about killing herself caused the mind of the witness to advert immediately to what was said the morning before. The real, true cause ought to be shown to the jury. The State says the remarks of Mary suggested the accused. We say they referred to actual, incontrovertible facts. If the dead girl's language of sadness and sorrow is to be cited, should not the true cause be shown? If Mary sighed and was sad because of an injury, cannot the real injury be shown instead of a fictitious one? The court ruled out the question, as the girl made no explanation of her state of mind at the very time.]

The question asked by Mr. Waller provoked in the press of the country more comment than was given to any single development in the trial, and with scarcely an exception the criticism was unfavorable to the lawyer. It was looked upon as an effort to produce a dramatic effect principally, and many conjectures were raised as to the real impression made upon the minds of the jury, who, as was subsequently ascertained after the trial had closed, were at the time strengthened in their favorable impression already formed toward Mrs. Hayden.

HON. GEO. H. WATROUS.

HON. SAML. F. JONES.

THE COUNSEL

HON. THOS. M. WALLER.

HON. LYNDE HARRISON.

MR. LYNDE HARRISON. January 14, 1880, made the opening argument for the State. His points are summed up as follows :

On the 3d day of September, 1878, a secret and foul murder was committed. In the peaceful Rockland village a fair young woman, standing on the threshold of life, one who had felt the blight of one man's wrong doing, was swiftly hurried out of the world into the dim and dread eternity. The people were aroused. It is said that when the tiger of India, escaping from a secret lair, seizes some child from an Indian village, the whole of the inhabitants of the place rush out and track him, if possible, into the recesses of the forest, and make it their business to destroy him. So all the people of Rockland village felt it incumbent on them to look into the cause of this murder. All the dreadful incidents of those three days were distinctly impressed upon the minds of those people. Clue after clue was picked up. Trace after trace was found. Track after track was investigated, and finally the machinery of the law took up this case, and it has been your duty and my duty to investigate and find out the truth.

First, we have proved the death of Mary Stannard. Then we have proved the cause of that death. We have called the doctors who saw the body and identified it, and the professors who have testified to what they have found in the body—the ninety grains of arsenic. Then comes the proof that Mr. Hayden, the accused, bought arsenic on that fatal morning. We claim to have shown how Mr. Hayden fabricated his defence by showing that the barn arsenic, which Hayden says he had bought, had been put there in order to account for arsenic which he admitted he had bought. We have proved the cause of death, the wound in her throat, and the possession by the accused of a sharp, small knife with which such a

wound might have been made. Then we have proved the time of
the murder. It must have been shortly after 3. Next we have
shown the motive of this crime. We have shown that Mary
Stannard had previously been the victim of another man ; that she
was then in a condition of body which might have produced the
same symptoms that she had previously had ; that she thought she
had those symptoms ; that she went home for the purpose of
obtaining assistance ; that she communicated with Mr. Hayden by
secret and private interviews. Then we proved that a man was seen
going toward the spot where the body was found, and we show that
every other person in the place can be accounted for except Herbert
H. Hayden at the time Mrs. Ward saw the man crossing the road.
Then we show the distance from the house to the wood lot, and
show that it would have been possible for a man to have passed from
one point to the other within the time when the prisoner was out of
sight of every mortal eye. Then we show the contradictions of Mr.
Hayden, and the blood spots found on his knife. Then we contradict many of the material statements of Mr. Hayden, and so the
end has been reached.

Under the laws of Connecticut the poisoning of a person or
deliberate killing is murder in the first degree. Another statute
provides that no such degree of murder shall be found unless the
evidence is equivalent to that of two credible eye-witnesses. It is
the duty of the jury in this case, if they consider the circumstantial
evidence equivalent, to find a verdict of guilty of murder in the first
degree. If not, they are at liberty to bring in a verdict in a lesser
degree. The State claims to have fully proved the murder by the
knife, arsenic and a blow on the head at the spot where the body
was found. The circumstances show that it was by a person in
whom the girl had confidence. Herbert H. Hayden is the man. He
had the motive, the means and the opportunity. He cannot satis-
factorily account for himself at the time of the girl's death, and has
involved himself by his statements and contradictions in endeavoring to do so. The girl could not have killed herself. No knife was
found. The nature of the wound in the throat proved it an
impossibility. There was no blood on her hands. Her declarations
to her sister show that she had a different motive in going into the
woods—to take " quick medicine."

Professor Johnson found nearly ninety grains of arsenic in Mary

Stannard's body. It permeated nearly all the organs. It could not have been introduced into the body after death, because the experts say that it could not have been carried to the brain by absorption between the time the body was buried and re-exhumed for the purpose of investigation. Professor Johnson found the seeds of blackberries in the dead girl's stomach. The remains of the blackberries were discovered in the stain of blood beneath the body. This showed conclusively that the action of the arsenic had induced vomiting, and the stomach had partially ejected the berries. Who bought the arsenic? Hayden. He secretly visits Middletown, starting very early in the morning, and returns secretly. He tells no one. He goes to a store where both employer and clerk say that they did not recognize him. He had passed a drug store in Madison on the previous day, before he had heard Mary's story, and had bought no poison. So far as is shown, he was the only person in Rockland who had the means of death in his possession, and he bought it just six hours before the death of the girl.

After a Middletown paper had announced that Mr. Hayden had been seen in Middletown, and had been to a drug store and bought some poison, the body was disinterred and examined for the purpose of determining whether it contained the same kind of poison that Hayden had bought. Then Mr. Hayden found it necessary to account for the ounce of arsenic. He accounted for it, how? On the 14th of September his premises were searched. On the 18th of September Sheriff Hull is asked : " Did you search the barn ?" and answered : "No ; I did not go there." Mr. Hayden was then led to infer naturally that no one had looked into the barn. The paper wrapper of the ounce of arsenic that he bought in Middletown cannot be produced. It is gone—scattered to the winds. He says he threw it into his shavings barrel. That is the first, last and only time that ever a sane man purchased poison, with the warning label upon it, and before he gets ready to use it takes it out of the original package, destroys the package, and puts the poison in a tin box on a beam in his barn, where any person might have found it, and, without warning of its dangerous nature, be likely to use it as sugar or salt. I do not think such a thing was ever done before, and we believe we have shown you that it was done for the purpose of fabricating a defence. After the 18th of September, when Mr. Hayden supposed the barn had not been searched, he goes upon the

stand and says the arsenic is in the tin box in his barn on the girder.
Now, let us see—was it there? General Wilcox says it was not
there. He carefully searched the barn on the 14th and did not find
it. He carefully felt along the girder, and swears that there was no
tin box there. Ten days after Wilcox's visit Mr. Hayden first said
that he had placed it there, and on the same night Talcott Davis
says he found it.

Mr. McKee, a druggist of Middletown, says that he bought two
pounds of arsenic on May 20, 1878, and two pounds in November.
During that time he sold two half-pounds to Druggist Tyler.
Tyler says he bought the last half-pound on June 24. Whatever
arsenic McKee sold in September and October was taken from the
same two-pound package as Tyler's half-pound. Sheriff Hull
bought some from him October 9. Tyler bought a ten-pound package in New York on July 27, but says he did not open it until all
the other was sold. This package was opened on October 9, when
Hull purchased an ounce. George A. Tyler swears that there was
none in the bottle, and that he then opened the fresh package. He
says that the last of the McKee arsenic was sold to a Mr. Colgrove
about the last of September. Colgrove called for an ounce, and
took what was left in the bottle. The experts discovered that the
package bought from McKee by Sheriff Hull and the Colgrove
arsenic were precisely alike. Tyler swears that there was none
placed in his jar between the time of his McKee purchase and the
opening of the package bought in New York. Hayden bought his
poison of Tyler on September 3. It was three weeks before Colgrove bought his. The Hayden arsenic must have topped the Colgrove arsenic in the jar, and it must certainly have been a portion
of the arsenic bought by Tyler from McKee. The experts testify
that the McKee, Colgrove and stomach arsenic were identical in the
size and proportion of crystals. The crystals of the barn arsenic
were much smaller and in a much larger proportion.

What was the motive of the murder? We have proved beyond
a reasonable doubt that Mary Stannard believed she was approaching maternity. She had some reason to believe so. Mrs. Studley
says that the Thursday, Friday and Saturday before she went home,
Mary was troubled in her mind; that she examined her, and confirmed her suspicions. She determined to send Mary home. She
told Mr. Studley that Mary was in trouble and proposed to go home

on account of it. Mary told Mr. Studley she was going home to
see Mr. Hayden. She told Mr. Studley she would like to have him
see Mr. Hayden. She did not want to see any other man than Mr.
Hayden. When she gets home she tells her sister what her
symptoms are. Her sister examined her, and reached the same
conclusion. Mary tells her sister that she has come home to see Mr.
Hayden, to get him to help her out of her trouble. She had been a
mother once before, and thought she knew the meaning of the
symptoms. All women in such trouble go to the man who caused
it. Mary did so. She wrote him the letter. If the letter had been
addressed to any other man than Mr. Hayden, she would have
sought that man. She was secretive about it. She asked her sister
to say nothing about it to her father, After two attempts she finally
saw Hayden on Monday afternoon in his barn. Two respectable
witnesses saw them enter the barn. Mrs. Hayden denies it, but there
was no reason why these two neighbors should perjure themselves.

Both these parties were poor, and concealment was important to
them. One thing they could do. Possibly an abortion might be
committed, so that no one could know of it but Mary and Mr.
Hayden. It is not the first time that such a method of escape has
presented a temptation to a man finding himself in such a fix. But
Mr. Hayden knew that such an effort sometimes fails, and death
follows, and then the woman lives long enough to tell who is the
author of her trouble. There was one other way to help him out,
and that was the crime of murder. That is safe, if not discovered,
so far as the world is concerned. Mary had confidence in somebody who gave her that ninety grains of arsenic. She could not
have taken such a quantity in her food. She must have taken it
believing it was medicine. She had confidence in the man to whom
she had given her virtue, and that man was Mr. Hayden. There is
no evidence of any other.

We have proved that there was a murder committed, that there
was a motive for committing it, and that the accused man had an
opportunity to commit it. What reply does he make? He denies
it, of course. The State has proved that Mary Stannard was
murdered, and that Herbert Hayden had a motive to commit that
murder, to prevent exposure of his relations to her ; that he had
private interviews with her ; that he had an appointment with her in
the woods ; that he did that murder, and that from that time he has

involved himself in a labyrinth of contradictions. Finally, it is
morally and absolutely impossible that any other man than Herbert
H. Hayden is guilty of the awful crime of sending the soul of Mary
E. Stannard, unprepared and unwarned, before the judgment seat
of her Maker.

SAMUEL F. JONES made the opening argument for the
defence:

Mr. Hayden was in Rockland, a young man of twenty-eight.
Up to the 3d of September his moral character was above reproach.
He was stationed over a little church. His career had been check-
ered. He had married early; he was struggling along, clothed in
poverty, and by the force of poverty and ill health he was settled in
Rockland. Hand in hand he and his wife were traveling over the
stony road of life. Rockland is not noted for its intellectual
products or for its love for the clergy. One day an event happened
that stirred the Stevens family. A little baby was born. It was
another addition to the Hayden family. Mrs. Luzerne Stevens was
not invited to officiate. Mrs. Hayden sent off a mile and a half for
Mrs. Talcott Davis. There was trouble in the Stevens household
over the little matter, and neither Mrs. Young (Luzerne Stevens's
sister) nor Mrs. Stevens would go over and see the baby. They
stood ready to pay off the little debt, and of course they could see
a hole in the barn on the day before the murder or on any other
day.

Go up the street. We find there Charles Stannard, a stupid,
clever old man. We have no suspicion that he is concerned in this
crime, and desire to cast none on him. His family consisted of
himself, Susan Hawley, Mary Stannard—when she was at home—
and Mary's little boy. The boy was a bone of contention. When
Susan came home from Ben Stevens's house, Mary was compelled to
go out to housework. She had one friend, however, in fair or foul
weather, and that was Mrs. Hayden. Mary reciprocated this feeling
and visited her frequently. On the day before the murder she said
that she could not stay in the house any longer without coming
down to see Mrs. Hayden. Who ran the Stannard house and
controlled it? Who stayed there nights and slept on an old sofa,
provided he did sleep there? Ben Stevens. Mr. Stannard was
poor—poorer even than Mr. Hayden. Stevens brought his rum

there Stevens brought his meat there to be cooked. Why? What was the magnet? Did he know any of the family? Oh, yes; he knew Susan Hawley. She had kept house for him, and when Mary left and she came home we find Ben Stevens taking the next train. He was worth $15,000 to $20,000. I don't think that Stannard knew or cared whether he slept on the sofa or elsewhere. Why is it that he was so intimate that he felt at liberty to lop down on a bed anywhere in the daytime? It is strange that he should leave his house, his son and daughter, for the purpose of sleeping on an old sofa in the Stannard house. Possibly, when Mary was not at home, Susan might sleep alone. The evidence as to the intimacy of Stevens with Susan is far more clear than any evidence of intimacy between Mary and Mr. Hayden. The body was found. Who could have had a motive? Susan Hawley sets the ball in motion. She points the clue. No other clue is followed. Suppose that the hounds had been put on Ben Stevens's track instead of Hayden's. There was four times the evidence against him. Who last saw her alive? Who, after she had gone into the woods, took the highway home in the hot afternoon instead of going in the shade? Who was it that said, afterward, false or true, that he had found a club with blood and hair on it? Ben Stevens. He did not remember it, but two of his old neighbors did remember it, and he himself acknowledged that he refused to talk with them because he was afraid of exposing himself. My God! suppose that Hayden had said that he had found a club covered with hair and blood, how that would have been thundered in your ears! Every means that ingenuity and malice can contrive has been used, not to discover the real perpetrator of the crime, but to convict Mr. Hayden. The prosecution tell you they wanted to be fair. Did they want to be fair when they secretly sent Dana to England and put a padlock on his mouth on his return, and placed a Yale lock on the mouths of his assistant professors? Why was this done? It was done in order that the defence might not make similar preparations to meet his testimony. Don't talk to me about fairness. " By authority of the State of Connecticut,' said Sheriff Hull, "I demand that you shall deliver up that arsenic under penalty of the law." Now you have got it let us hope you don't tamper with it. Why keep your objects a secret! Why not say: " Mr. Jones, we have found arsenic ; you select your expert and we will select ours, and see whether we cannot get at the

bottom of this crime." That would have been fair. Thank heaven
that Hull did not get hold of the clothing! Had he done so, God
alone knows what the prosecution would have found!

As to General Wilcox, who furnishes the much needed testimony
that the tin box of arsenic was not in the barn when Mr. Hayden
says it was, where did he get his title of General? He is a profes-
sional detective, and his testimony that he examined that barn on
September 14, 1878, is, I believe, a coined and manufactured lie.
Why was it furnished at so late a day? Because it was a little link
in the testimony that was wanted, and its introduction was not made
until after General Wilcox had had an opportunity to go up and
examine the barn, and inform himself on the appearance of it. But
did he know anything of the condition of that barn on September
14, when he says he was there? On the contrary, he was mistaken
about what was there, for the very reason that he did not go until
long after the time referred to by Mr. Hayden. It is very strange
that he kept quiet about his important testimony until a very recent
time, while he knew it was an important point for the State. The
explanation of his delay is that he had not made any such visit
until about the time that he swore to it.

As to the alleged letter of Mary Stannard to Susan Hawley, Mr.
Jones argued that there was no evidence that it was Mary's letter,
and he asked the Court to charge that, even if it was Mary
Stannard's letter, it could not be used against Mr. Hayden, or as
evidence of his relations to her. As to the blood on Mr. Hayden's
knife, he scouted the idea that Mr. Hayden would have kept that
knife in the way he did keep it if he had used it to commit a
murder. As to the testimony of Mrs. Ward that she saw a man,
which the State claims was Mr. Hayden, going toward the spot
where Mary was murdered, there is not the slightest pretence that
she identified Mr. Hayden. The State makes the absurd claim that
it must have been Mr. Hayden because it was nobody else. Is it
likely that Mr. Hayden, who was about to commit a murder, would
put himself in the way to be seen?

Passing to the testimony of Susan Hawley, Mr. Jones began by
asking the Court to charge that nothing in her declarations of what
was said to her by Mary Stannard prior to the time that Mary went
into the woods, and as to the purpose for which she was going there
to meet Mr. Hayden, could be received by the jury as evidence

against Mr. Hayden. He claimed that the testimony to prove where Mr. Hayden was and why he went there must come from some other source.

As Mr. Jones began to criticise Susan Hawley's character and testimony rather severely, Susan got up and left the court with downcast mien and flushed face, accompanied by her half sister, Imogene Stannard. She had been proved guilty of several lies. She said she lied to her father when she said Mary had come home because her boy was troublesome. Then it was exceedingly improbable that, when Mary Stannard was going away from home to get an abortion committed at 2 o'clock, she should have made an arrangement to come back and help do the baking, and then after that to go out and take a walk.

The State has been literally plundered by the witnesses for the prosecution. With all the testimony that the prosecution could rake together, the public mind must be kept fired by outside influences. Many of the jurymen must come from New Haven, and, if possible, they must be prejudiced. So it was published to the world that a tiny piece of steel that would fit a nick in the Hayden knife was found in the dead girl's gullet. The prosecution deny that they were responsible for the publication. But who did it? One who acted in their interest, an enemy to Mr. Hayden. His purpose was self-evident. It was to convict Mr. Hayden. So much for the efforts of the prosecution.

The State started out with a superabundance of theories. Some were stillborn ; others had a very brief existence. The boot-heel theory died from an overdose of public policy. Then there was the line-of-sight theory. Mrs. Hayden has testified that she saw her husband's carriage in the road above the spring. Surveyor Butler, on behalf of the prosecution, swore that the line of sight was from fourteen to forty feet in the air at that point Fortunately the jury went out to Rockland, and from actual observation convinced themselves that Mrs. Hayden was correct. The case was started on the theory that the girl had killed herself because she was about to become a mother. Dr. Matthewson made an examination, and found no such evidence. There was not a scintilla of proof that Mr. Hayden had ever been intimate with her. Take the stories about the oyster supper. If he was going to see Mary, would he follow right on the heels of her brother and sister ? He had given

her no presents, and no meetings were proved. Above all, she was
in no danger of becoming a mother.

Now, gentlemen, I want you to suppose that the girl was pure.
Suppose that Mr. Hayden had been criminally intimate with her
five months before that time, the 3d of September ; suppose that
she thought she was about to become a mother, and that she went
through a supposed hole in the barn and had a private interview
with the accused, she would say : "Mr. Hayden, I am in trouble."
He would reply : "What makes you think so ?" In answering, she
acknowledged that an infallible sign of nature pointed otherwise.
Do you suppose that, after receiving this information, any man in
God's world would have rushed off to Middletown to buy arsenic to
put the girl out of the way ? Even if her suspicions were correct,
he would have given her fifteen dollars and sent her over to New
Haven for a special purpose. The theory will not hold water. If
he took that girl's life he must have done it because she was trying
to levy blackmail upon him ; and if you prove the girl a liar your
case is gone, bob and sinker. The prosecution, through Mr. Root,
tells you that Mr. Studley said that Mary was approaching maternity.
Justice Wilcox, before whom Mrs. Studley testified, denies this. To
be sure, Mary was sent away from Mr. Studley's for some reason. It
may be because her child made trouble. If so, it is not competent
for us to prove it. The prosecution may do so ; we cannot. Mary
Stannard gave this reason to Susan and to her father, and Edgar
Studley admitted that he had said that her boy was the worst boy
that he ever saw. Why did she leave her clothes at Mrs. Studley's ?
Did she have anything to do with anybody in that house ? Perhaps
Mother Studley had good reasons of her own for wishing her to
return home. I shall ask the Court to charge that the testimony of
Mrs. Studley, as detailed by the reporter, Mr. Root, the testimony of
Susan Hawley in reference to the statement of the deceased girl as
to what Mary believed to be her condition, was admitted for the
purpose of showing, what Mary supposed her physical condition to
be, and cannot be used by the jury in finding whether Hayden was
the cause of the supposed condition, or whether Hayden committed
the crime for which he is upon trial. You can't get testimony in
for one purpose and use it for another.

Mr. Jones then analyzed the evidence that the State had
furnished bearing on the guilt of Hayden. He hoped that, even if

a man had a domestic in his house, he could visit it after nightfall
to put his children to bed without being accused of harboring an
improper purpose. No feeling on Mr. Hayden's part against Mary
Stannard was shown. He was not even at the spot where the
murder was committed, and he was not seen either going to or
returning from that spot. He did not try to avoid an investigation.
He has neither said nor written anything that can fasten suspicion
upon him. There was no evidence of guilt on his clothes. There
were no footprints. There was nothing in his conduct, either before
or after the girl's death, that could tend to criminate him. Summed
up, the evidence for the prosecution amounts to this : That somebody said that somebody else said that Herbert H. Hayden was
criminally intimate with Mary Stannard. There was no occasion
for him to tell the story concerning the purchasing of the arsenic.
The druggist, Tyler, did not know him. The presence of the
arsenic in the girl's stomach could not tell against him. Any
designing man could have placed it there after death. Any man in
Dr. White's confidence could have put half a pound of the poison
in the stomach while it was canned in the Yale Medical College.
Professor Johnson, an honest expert, would not undertake to say
when it was placed there. Stannard or Stevens could have done it.
Does it look as though Hayden purchased the arsenic with an
improper purpose? If he meant to kill the girl, he could not have
contemplated it before she had told him of her situation. Yet he
was talking with Thomas Pendelow about buying arsenic a full
month before her death. If he is guilty, why should he go to the
very drug store which he was in the habit of patronizing? He
would have been in some by-place, getting a little boy to purchase
the arsenic for him. His conduct on the afternoon of the murder,
reading his wife's letter, lying on the floor and playing with his
child, shows that he could not have had murder in his heart.
Then, again, Mr. Hayden is an educated man. Whoever put that
arsenic in the girl's stomach was not an educated man. He had no
idea of a fatal dose. We don't know how it got into her stomach,
but we can easily conceive that it might have been given to her at
dinner. Mary Stannard's letter to Susan Hawley was no proof
against Mr. Hayden. Susan's refusal to write her sister's name in
court was a suspicious circumstance. The signature was Mary
Stanard, and only one ' n " at that. The girl's name was Mary E.

Stannard. Which would be the most likely to leave out the "E" and the "n," Susan Hawley or Mary E. Stannard? The name in the postscript was originally written "Hazley" or "Hayley," and this circumstance has not been explained.

[The letter referred to, which Susan Hawley, half-sister of Mary Stannard, testified was sent to her by Mary to be delivered to Mr. Hayden, was never given to him, because, the witness said, Mary came home and said she would see him herself. Susan testified that she gave the Hayden letter back to Mary, who destroyed it. But Susan kept the letter addressed to herself, and the only thing in it of importance in the trial was the following postscript, written with a lead pencil :

do not let farther see this I want you to give this letter to Mr. hayden and don't let any body see it and I will tell you what it is for some day. You give it to him your self,

Don't read this to farther

The name "hayden" was not clear; the "y" looked so much like a "z;" the "d" was a distinct "l;" and there was a loop below the last letter "n" as if it might have been first written a "y."]

Mr. Jones then paid his respects to the professors. "Scientific evidence," he said, "is the most dangerous of all evidence." He read extracts from various authorities to prove this assertion. "If any scamp," he said, "wants to sell a silver mine, he will dig for Yale College to get expert testimony." He then scathed Mr. Waller for his conduct toward Mrs. Hayden in asking her whether she would deny her God to save her passionately-loved husband. Referring to the Rev. Mr. Gibbs, he accused him of lying, and said that he pitied the miserable creature.

After solemnly impressing upon the jury their duty to give the accused the benefit of every doubt, he said that the testimony of Ben Stevens is contradicted by at least fifteen different witnesses. Mr. Jones next considered the alleged contradictions of Mr. Hayden. He accounted for the apparent length of time consumed by Mr. Hayden in his work in the wood lot by saying that he was not working, as the witnesses for the prosecution were, to see how quickly he could do it, but was working leisurely, as a man naturally would in doing such work, with nothing specially to hurry him.

With reference to the apparent contradiction of Mr. Hayden in the testimony of Mr. Eldridge that Mr. Hayden had, in conversation with him, shown a knowledge of Mary Stannard's condition, Mr. Jones said: "Even if Mr. Hayden did know as much about that as Mr. Eldridge says he did, it is really in his favor, because then he had less motive to kill the girl. The more you can make him acquainted with the actual physical condition of Mary Stannard, the less motive he had to kill her."

In conclusion, he said : "Take the history of this man's life; take his family surroundings ; take his family condition ; take his conduct at Madison ; take his conduct when the body was found ; take his conduct in the purchase of the arsenic and everything connected with it. The idea that he had anything criminal in his mind when the arsenic was bought is preposterous. I leave him with you twelve honest men, and I leave him with confidence, but not without invoking upon his head that prayer which I once heard invoked on another : 'May God grant to thee a safe deliverance.'"

THOMAS M. WALLER followed in an address to the jury for the State:

We are trying for the murder of that frail girl a minister of God's gospel. And the presumption is that, because he is a minister, he may be innocent. I say a minister, and I say, gentlemen, that it is a profession that every decent man in the community will bow to. I respect the poor minister as well as the rich one ; as well they that work in the rocky places as those who labor in the crowded cities.

> "A man he was to all the country dear,
> And passing rich on forty pounds a year."

But, gentlemen, all ministers are not good. God pity them. There are those that are unchaste and that commit crimes. When Christ selected his twelve disciples there were two that betrayed him ; Peter, who was weak, and Judas the betrayer. None can tell today whether the bad men in God's flock are the least or the greater. If you look upon this testimony as I do, I trust you will find a verdict in accordance with the facts.

Mary arrives home on that pleasant September afternoon. She does not go to Mr. Hayden's house, because she knows he is not at home. She starts early on Monday morning, but she sees Mrs. Hayden and not the man, and Mrs. Hayden says she tells her that she wanted to see the baby. Back home she goes ; between ten and eleven o'clock she returns, but does not find him at home at this time. At three o'clock she finds another excuse to go down to Hayden's. She has been there twice before. Does she see Hayden? Yes, she does. She goes with him to the barn, and Mrs. Young sees her go. She goes to see him alone. Henrietta Young tells the truth, and Rachel Stevens tells the truth, though it may wring your hearts. She meets him in the barn. You can hear her say to him : "I am pregnant; my breasts are hard ; what can you do for me?" He thinks of three things. One is confession ; but a confession will damn him forever ; if he confesses, he loses his place and damns his wife and children. What next? He thinks of abortion ; but oh! the danger of exposure! The devil wrestles with him ; it must be death ! death ! death ! He hears her story. He says to himself, I will do no work tomorrow. A man says, I want you to work for me. He says, I can't go tomorrow, I will go Wednesday. He leaves his house on Tuesday morning without telling his wife where he is going. He takes a molasses jug and starts for Durham. Does he ask for arsenic there ? No ; he goes to Middletown. Will he see any one that knows him for a minister ? No. Will he know the druggist ? No. He will get his arsenic where he is not known. He meets a Rockland boy ; what now ? The devil puts it in his head to go to Mr. Burton's. Well, he is in doubt about that girl's condition, and he will ask a doctor. He sees Dr. Bailey, and he don't tell him that he has got the girl in a family way. He inquires about the symptoms of his wife. Back he goes on the Middletown road, and he stops at Stannard's. Uncle Ben is there ; Charles Stannard is there ; how shall he see Mary ? He asks for a drink of water and gets it. Mary starts for the spring ; now he will get an opportunity to speak with her. He puts his children in the buggy and starts down the hill ; he meets Mary near the spring. He wants a drink of water, does he ? Mary cannot lift that little pail ; he could not bend over and lift it up. No ; he clambers over the oats in front of him, gets out and talks with Mary. He says he did not. What does Mary say ? She tells Susan that Hayden has been to Middletown and got some "quick medicine," and he is to meet her at the Big Rock. Do you believe him when he says he did not know that that monarch rock stood up there in the woods? Yet he leads the men around the pathway after the murder. Well, Mary says she is going to get blackberries, and we leave her for awhile, and go back to the spring, and go home with that man. He has the arsenic. Who knows where it is ? Nobody but he. He is to meet that girl at one o'clock. He will start out innocently on his bloody errand, and he leaves at one o'clock. He says it was later, but he had previously told six men on a jury panel that he started at one o'clock. If he said so at that time he thought so ; and not knowing what he would finally have to meet. Now, how does he go ? He does not tell his wife that he has got the knife or the arsenic in his pocket. Mrs. Hayden says he did not take the knife. She wanted to use it. She says also that she had a letter to write that afternoon. Did she write that letter and peel the pears on that afternoon ? No, gentlemen. He says he starts out with his children, but nobody sees them.·

Let us follow the steps of him who was doomed to go over the precipice, where the devil had thrust him. He starts with children, and, when they get to a certain corner, he turns them back. His wife sees him, if she was at the window. He will, of course, go to the wood lot if his wife is looking. He will not turn back while she is sitting at the window. He gets there, and thinks he will pass the time in throwing up the wood until his wife has turned from the window. She is gone, and he turns back again through the bushes, and, quick as a flash, he crosses the road and is out of sight in the woods. He goes to meet the woman that is pregnant ; he goes to meet the woman to whom he is to give the arsenic. He has left his home, kissed his wife, and he that has put on the vestments of chastity is about to kill the woman who is a mother. It is half-past two, and he meets her. Oh, Mary Stannard ! if you could walk into the court-room and give the details of that interview between you and your murderer ! He takes out the arsenic ; he does not place it on the point of a knife ; she takes it and a burning seizes upon her. You can hear her talk to him. He says: Don't cry out, Mary ; the pains and pangs you are suffering are the pains and pangs of abortion. The look of the man may have frightened her; and, as she looked into his face, she may have seen that he intended murder; and she screamed. A moment after she was dead. She falls, writhing in the agonies of death ; and he takes from his pocket a keen, sharp knife ; his sleeves are rolled up, and he thrusts that knife into her throat. The girl is dead, and the devil himself must have been amazed. Now, what does the murderer do? He rushes from the place, and at the nearest brook washes the knife; washes it and it is clean. He looks at his shirt and there is no blood upon it. There is a little dirt in the groove of the knife, and the least particle of blood remains there. There are only fifteen corpuscles, but those few corpuscles tell of his guilt. But he flees. God's thunder is rolling in the skies, the voice of the same God that thundered on Sinai. Where does he go? He must keep away from everybody ; he must get back to the wood lot. The devil is behind him, the sheriff is behind him, the gallows is behind him, and he hurries back.

But they say, gentlemen, we have not proven any intimacy. No, we haven't. No one ever saw him with the woman. She lived in his house six months, and do you say that crime could not have been committed? What do we prove about that oyster supper? Does any one contradict Charles Hawley and Imogene Stannard? One good woman swears that she was at that supper, and she knows Hayden could not have been away. Yet she admits he might have been up stairs forty minutes and she not have known it. Then comes another man who swears that he saw Hayden at just eleven o'clock, yet he cannot tell where his wife was or what he was doing. Was there any reason for Hayden to go home and take care of these children that night? No. Mary was there ; she loved the children and they loved her. Weak, feeble excuse.

Twelve years ago, gentlemen, there would have been differences in this case. The prisoner could not have testified ; the wife could not have testified. I have been charged with cruelty by some of the newspapers. If you have not read it there is no use for me to speak of it. I say now, gentlemen, what I said then, that, if a woman believes her husband to be innocent, it is her duty to say so. If my wife is likely to starve for want of bread, I will steal it for her. God himself would not punish me for it. One word more. It is cruel for a woman to testify. If a wife should commit perjury for the sake of her husband, I don't know whether she could be punished or not, but I know she ought not to be. When they ask me to punish a woman in my county for committing perjury to save the life of her husband, they will have to send to New Haven county for somebody to do it. The poor woman has been contra- dicted by several witnesses. The defence have charged conspiracy to murder on the women of Stannard's family. They have charged it on Ben Stevens. What is the motive for Uncle Ben to commit the murder? Not that he has got the woman in the family way · he is too old for that. There is no reason. The counsel on the other side say that he wanted the room in the bed with Susan Hawley that Mary Stannard occupied. So he went up into the woods cut her throat, and gave her the arsenic. What folly! Ben Stevens is out of the case. Then they have brought up Hazlett, and he has gone out of the case. What was there for a motive? I can see how the devil can take a man and lead him on and on; but how such a murder can be committed, and then come into court and try to throw it on some one else, is beyond my comprehension.

Gentlemen, I leave the case in your hands. If anything has crawled into that circle of yours that you feel to influence you, go home, and, if you never prayed before, pray now that you may be forgiven. Remember that unpunished murder takes something from the security of the people, and when the jury allow a guilty man to escape they add to the insecurity of the people. I cannot understand why the law is so, that the counsel for the prisoner can have the last plea, but such is the case. Do your duty, gentlemen, and, if you are led to a verdict of murder in the second degree, approach your duty without fear. Out of that group came the victim, and if you wait to punish criminals without affecting the wife and children you will wait forever. If you wait to see guilt in the countenance of a prisoner tried for murder, you will wait forever. Gentlemen, you must do your duty, and let not woman's tears deprive you of judgment. Approach your duty faithfully and leave the consequences to God.

GEORGE H. WATROUS, of the prisoner's counsel, made the closing appeal to the jury:

The vastness of this testimony, as compared with the littleness of the results, can be best expressed by a school-boy's quotation from Horace: "Verily the mountains are in the throes of child-birth and a very small mouse is delivered." Truly there has been great labor, and what has been the result? What do you know now about who killed Mary Stannard?

On the 3d of September, 1878, Mary Stannard was killed. Her dead body, cold and motionless, was found the afternoon of that day

up in the woods. That she committed suicide is not, in my
judgment, probable. That she might have committed suicide is not
at all impossible. She might have made the blow on the head herself she might have taken the arsenic. But I do not lay much
stress upon the theory that the girl committed suicide. Calling it
murder, then, you are to look for the facts connected with that
murder—not probabilities, but facts. Who caused that death?

The State hang their case upon the theory that Mary thought she
was pregnant. Take the rule and apply it with common sense. I
tell you Mary Stannard's condition did not furnish a motive. She
was no more in the family way than either of you twelve men. Sad!
why, she was always sad. She was always sad when these periodi-
cals came upon her. There was a marked diminution in the flow of
her spirits at these times. Said good Mrs. Hayden: "She was
always sad at these times." Mary supposed a good deal at these
times. She was depressed in spirits.

They, say she must have been in trouble because she wrote a
letter. There wasn't a sign in Guilford found by Mrs. Studley, and
not a sign in Rockland found by the expert Susan ; and yet they
say she wrote a letter to Susan and enclosed one for Hayden,
alleging paternity ; she may have written this letter and she may not
have done so.

Isn't it singular they didn't lay in a letter, incontestably in
Mary's hand, as a comparison? No ; you've got Susan's testimony
that Mary said she wrote the letter. I wish we had something with
which to make a comparison. Beyond a reasonable doubt there is
no motive shown on the part of the accused. That letter I don't
believe Mary wrote. If she couldn't spell a whole word in the
dictionary right, she would spell her own name right ; she wouldn't
leave out the "E" or the "n." The letter is important ; if it
doesn't show motive against Mr. Hayden, it shows motive against
the guilty man, and it was written to shield him. It is a singular
fact that Mary, so overwhelmed and compelled to write a letter to her
alleged seducer, would sit down and write a letter to Susan Hawley.
It is signed Mary Stanard—they call it Stannard. I call your attention
to the fact that it is only "Stanar"—there is no "d." "Don't let
father see it." See what? The fact that she was unwell? "I want
you to give this letter to Mr. Hayden." Hayden they make it ; I
can't make it. It is either Hazley or Hayley beyond all doubt.

The writing of the letter was admitted for the purpose of show-ing intimacy, not improper, but such relations as show it possible for her to write a letter to him on some subject. The weight to be attached to it is as if I should write a letter to a client in New York, and he, showing it, should claim it as showing the relations between him and me. Some say that she went to Hayden's house Sunday ; some say she didn't ; I don't care if she did. Henrietta Young, the two-story woman, says she saw her ; Mrs. Luzerne Stevens says she saw her. I don't think it wrong for a girl to go and see her pastor's newly-born child ; so I shall cast my vote for Susan this time, and say Mary left the house at an early hour. Mrs. Hayden sympathized with the unfortunate girl, partly because she was unfortunate—God bless her for it—and she wanted to see the child. Is the husband of this woman to be hung because Mary brought the ugly boy home, and because she went to draw some comfort in her distress ? But the State says you must read between the lines. She thought she was in trouble, because she went to see Mrs. Hayden and tried to see Mr. Hayden, but couldn't. Didn't she know Mr. Hayden wasn't there ? The State say she was familiar with the house. She knew his habits ; she knew he had been preaching in South Madison for a year or more ; she knew he wasn't there ; she had been a servant in the house. But they say she went again because she hadn't seen Mr. Hayden. About ten o'clock her father sent her down to Stevens's for butter. "There is no dispute about it, he did," says the State. "But look between the lines." Although her father sent her for butter she went some-where else. This is as absurd as the other. Impelled by a sense of filial duty, she went on the errand. She wasn't sent by her father to see Hayden ; she knew he wasn't at home at that hour. I pray not to visit upon Mary the many foolish and wicked things this half-sister Susan has stated she did. She didn't get the butter, and on the way back she stopped at Hayden's to rest. These attacks upon this man show how hard driven some one is to prove somehow or other he is guilty. Mary's father said : "Stop at Mr. Hayden's and get the rake." Sometimes things happen to fit their environment. Aren't these sufficient motives for her visits ?

Give what degree of credence the testimony of Hayden deserves, but don't throw it entirely aside. In that house was Mr. Hayden, Mrs. Hayden and her young child. Mr. Hayden had just put up his horse and sat reading his paper. Now, I don't believe Mrs. Hayden invented these facts. Mary came to the door; Mr. Hayden got up after the usual salutation. Mary said: "Father wants to borrow your rake." He said: "Yes, you can have it." He laid down his paper and Mary took the baby from Mrs. Hayden and sat down with it. Both Mr. and Mrs. Hayden testify to this; and Mary herself would say so if she could look down from heaven. He went to the barn and got the rake. Mary saw him coming back and said: "Mr. Hayden's coming; what shall I do with the baby?" She said put it in the crib, and she placed it there, stepped out on the veranda, took the rake, said: "Are you in a hurry for it?" or some such thing, and passed on. Now, gentlemen, this is true, or Mrs. Hayden is the fiend that my very learned friend suggested upon one memorable occasion which you and I remember. Did Mrs. Hayden and Mary rise and go to the door together as he came from the barn? There is no doubt about it. If I allowed myself to stand here and argue that Mrs. Hayden would not commit perjury, I would have less respect for myself than now. Perjury? Thank God, you have seen her! Read it in the lineaments of her face? You might as well read Hebrew there. I beg her pardon for discussing the question. If she is honest, gentlemen, the State's case falls. That meeting was indispensable to the events of the succeeding day. Credit the story told by that honest woman, and I care not what you think of the rest of the case.

Now, look a moment at that question of whether he did the deed. Thus far the question of Mary's belief as to her physical condition had entered into the treatment by the speaker. My eloquent and learned friend, soaring in his eloquence on pinions high, has pictured out a scene of felicity in the cow pasture, at which he suggests the foundation might have been laid for a motive for the crime of murder. Possibly—I say possibly—such a meeting was had. But it is not to weigh a second here. Any one of the jury may meet a woman in a pasture lot sometime; but the State draws a purely imaginary picture in its struggle to find symptoms of improper intercourse. My client went to Middletown. He bought arsenic. That is true. He may be a fool for telling it before anybody knew of it, but the fact is so. Rats infested the barn. Mr. Hayden's wife, however, was averse to having arsenic in the house. But by and by the choice things, the preserves, were spoiled by the rats, and then the pastor got up courage to buy arsenic. He went to Middletown, coupling with the arsenic errand various other objects connected with his household. Oh! but they say he didn't tell his wife. One reason was because he wasn't certain about going himself. Another was that she was ill and weak. He did not decide to go to Middletown until after he had reached Durham. Look at the whole aspect of the trip and the man's conduct. Here features were alluded to as showing every indication of innocence—of any thought of crime. Why, if the thought of secresy struck him later on the journey, would he have stopped at Burton's for the tools, or been free and social with the charcoal peddler, and, as it were, leave tracks of his guilt? He certainly took most extraordinary freedom for a man about to commit an atrocious crime. Was there anything in his course or behavior throwing the least shadow of secresy about the trip! If he had the thousandth part of the intellect my friends feel obliged to credit him with in order to make a case, would he have laid himself open in this way? I have frequently tried criminal causes, but I have never in my experience—and you, gentlemen, will bear me out—had a case where the innocent actions of a man were marshaled as evidence of guilt, or when broad daylight conduct was construed as evidence of guilt. But he came down the street toward Stannard's. Is there a man in this panel who thinks Hayden stopped there in pursuance of an arrangement with Mary Stannard? The State does not pretend that he stopped there for a glass of water. He was too near home for that. What did he stop there for? As he came down the road he says his little girl said: "Papa, I want to ride home." Is that so? Susan confirms it. The old man Stannard confirms it, and it is one of those things that Ben Stevens does not happen to deny. Now, it would be a mighty lucky coincidence for the State that the children were there, as a part of the design. But that won't do. Was Mrs. Hayden a party to the arrangement for killing Mary Stannard? No one has the hardihood to charge or insinuate that. No; Mary was up the way by the Hayden house, and the children were sent by her to go to the Stannard house to come home with father. Could that father, so tender, so touching to those children, have included his offspring in a plan for murder? A man carrying a soul like that man has in his jacket capable of such a damnable scheme? It is not to be believed. What chance for an assignment with Mary

Stannard? But a wink or a nod is suggested. Even the facile
Susan, who could read between the lines of Mary's visits to the
Hayden house, even she saw nothing, no wink, no nod, no snapping
of the fingers, and even Ben Stevens cannot say so. Why did Mary
go privately? There was occasion for water in that family just at
that particular time. Mary goes after the water, and, on the way
home, Hayden sees her and the cool, pure water, and was his thirst
any the less, and why not allay it? But he got out of the wagon to
take a drink, and the State says he ought to be hung for it. If he
has got the gallantry to get out of the wagon, instead of the infernal
meanness of making her lift the heavy ten-quart pail of water up to
him, he is guilty of murder, my friend says. Ah! my friend says
he is a murderer because he got out, instead of being a great lazy
lubber and forcing the girl to raise it up to him by main strength.
But, it is said, we have caught Hayden in a lie. I can conceive that
a man might tell a lie about a matter of that sort and yet be perfectly
innocent. He might reason: I am suspected; I'll throw it away.
Away it goes. On second thought he says: Why, how stupid, it
was. They certainly know I went to Middletown. They say I
went after "quick medicine," and it will be easily found out that I
bought arsenic at Tyler's drug store. I shall be asked where it is. I
say I've thrown it away. I'll get some more and replace that first
quantity. Innocent men do just such foolish things. Take the
case of a man near Dublin, who saw the dead body of a friend on
the ground with a fork in his heart. He drew it out. As he did he
became covered with the blood. The thought flashed upon him: I
shall be hung. I'll out of this. He took off the clothes, he burned
them up and pretended to be sick. That man was tried for the
murder of that comrade, and by good fortune the only man who
knew how that death occurred got himself on that panel and stood
between his innocent friend and death. I don't say that Hayden
destroyed the arsenic, but I cite this to illustrate the point I named.
No; the fact is that he put it in the barn, and the next day intended
to make use of it for the purpose he bought it for. As to the
arsenic differing and being distinctly separate and distinguishable, I
say an ambitious expert I am afraid of, and an unscrupulous expert
I dread. They hold the keys to nature's arcana. The things that
they know are doled out to ordinary mortals as they see fit. You
know so much of these locked-up secrets of nature as those learned

men see fit to tell you. But if gentlemen of this jury do not know
that fact makes it absolutely necessary that such testimony comes
under the best possible guarantees. I say it is dreadful to swear
away a life in the chance that this may differ from that or that.

No, gentlemen, Mr. Hayden is not contradicted on this matter.
I will conclude briefly. You, gentlemen, must not conclude that
nobody bought arsenic except Hayden: I want to speak a word
about the knives. If Hayden didn't have that knife with him he
didn't cut that girl's throat. Now, did he have that knife? His
wife says he didn't. Mrs. Talcott Davis and her daughter heard
him ask for it the next day. Mrs. Hayden tells such a wonderfully
clear story about the whereabouts of that knife that I must allude to
it. Mr. Watrous rehearsed the pear peeling with the use of that
knife and the other intrinsic evidences he claimed of the perfect
inherent truth of her story, even without the support of the other
witnesses. If that little story is true, gentlemen, have you a
moment's doubt that the man is innocent?

Mr. Watrous now powerfully summed up. Look, he said, at the
accused saying good bye to his wife as he goes, as the State would
have us believe, on an errand of murder. He gives her a loving
good bye, and says here's a kiss for you, darling, while on the way.
See him going by the Burr barn and by the turnip patch, scudding
along, going to murder Mary Stannard. He is going quickly, as if
to say : I am going to commit a terrible murder and get back as
quick as I can ; and, with this mission before him, he says, my dear
wife, and leaves her an affectionate good-bye. This the State is
driven to by its theory. See the man coming back from his terrible
problem of murder, with his little boys by his side, turning about in
the way and throwing a kiss to the mother as she sits by the window
with another child, a new born babe, in her arms. I say to you
was ever such tender conduct put on? Again they say to him : You
changed your clothes, did you? How about that conduct? Ah! he
tells the simple, natural fact. He says : I changed them. What
does he do with them? Throws them down on the chamber floor.
They were not washed, by a Providence of God, and they showed
no evidence of guilt. Nobody contradicts him at all in this except
the ubiquitous, long-jointed Luzerne Stevens. Mr. Watrous here,
his voice rising and with the deepest feeling in his tones, repudiated
the idea of a verdict in the second degree, stigmatizing it as a com-

promise and subterfuge. Mr. Hayden was either guilty clear to the bottom or innocent clear to the top. If Mr. Hayden killed that girl, he should suffer the utmost penalty of the law, and it will be just. But do not be wheedled or cajoled as to a compromise, and I say that Mr. Hayden is either guilty of the crime or entitled to be acquitted. This my client demands, and most justly. If satisfied that there is a reasonable doubt that this man did the deed, he must be acquitted, he must go free. If not satisfied, he must go up. My task is done. Gentlemen of the jury, this man's life is in your hands. You have got to decide whether that man there is to live or die. You are to settle whether that woman henceforth is to be a widow with the stinging disgrace that her husband was a murderer. You are to settle whether those bright little children shall have a father whose name they cannot mention but with a blush of shame. You, gentlemen, are to say whether that devoted father, whose attention and devotion we have all admired, shall be sent from this court-house, disgraced, and the boy, the pride of his household and the one selected to be a minister to God's people on earth, shall die a malefactor. And that loving old mother, into whose honest face you could not look but with sympathy. She looks and waits upon your lips for the decision which shall either make her happy again with her son, her innocent son free, or make her remaining days ten-fold more wretched because convicting him of a terrible crime. So do that, in the hereafter, there will be no little lips lisping, as they point to you with scorn : "There's one of the twelve men who hung an innocent man who was charged with crime under suspicious circumstances." So do your whole duty, not alone to the whole circle of friends to this man, who are legion, but to this immediate circle gathered around this poor man ; to this devoted woman who has stood and watched with him through the progress of this trial. I speak particularly of this whole family group, and of those little ones who are not here to witness these scenes. So do your duty with that group that their hearts shall not be broken ; so that this much persecuted, much wronged man will be restored with what is left of life and joy after this long cruelty. So do and act that that man shall go back to liberty, to his wife, his father, his mother, and darling little ones, and I am sure God Almighty, reigning above, will record that verdict in the great book to your everlasting honor.

THE TRIAL CLOSED.

The great trial, after the charge of Judge Park following the arguments of counsel, was left in the hands of the jury on Friday, January 16, 1880, and intense excitement prevailed in and about the New Haven court-house during that day and the succeeding days until the case was disposed of. The jury were kept in constant charge by Sheriff Byxbee, having food and lodging provided for them. What their deliberations amounted to no one could accurately conjecture, though there were many rumors current, and finally it was generally believed that the delay in reporting was due to the refusal of a single man to agree to a verdict of acquittal, and so it proved. Eleven jurors speedily agreed upon a verdict, but the twelfth man declined to go with them ; and it transpired that he refused from the start to accept the testimony of Mr. and Mrs. Hayden as of any account in the case, though basing his entire opinion upon the purely circumstantial evidence upon which his associates were convinced of Mr. Hayden's innocence. There has been some severe criticism of this single juror's conduct, but it is all a matter for his own conscience, and lies between himself and Him who understands the moving motives of all men.

The jury finally reported, Monday night, after being out nearly eighty-two hours, that they could not agree, and they were discharged. The eleven, as they left their seats, warmly greeted both Mr. and Mrs. Hayden, and the scene was of the most touching character.

. A few days later it was agreed that Mr. Hayden should be released, but whether upon his own recognizance or upon a nominal bond was left open. With but little delay State Attorney Doolittle permitted a bond, given by Mr. Watrous and Mr. I. M. Hubbard, of the counsel for the defence, to be taken, and thereupon Mr. Hayden was released from custody.

Before leaving jail Mr. Hayden was visited by a reporter, who printed the following account of the interview :

"Come in," he said, in a pleasant tone of voice. "I'm sure you're heartily welcome. You must excuse the disorder of the apartment. I am packing up, preparatory to departure."

He removed his shaving cup from his trunk, to make a seat for Jesse Shaw, his brother-in-law.

"I want to ask you some questions, and ask permission to print your answers," we said.

He smiled. "That's honestly put," he replied. "I don't know that I have anything to say. Perhaps enough has already been said in the newspapers. I have read reports of conversations in some of them that have never taken place. My friends feel more hurt about them than I do."

He was then asked what he proposed to do when released. His replies were manly, and devoid of religious affectation. During his long trial he has borne himself more like a stout-hearted man in trouble than like a representative of the church. If he has trusted in God, he has trusted in Him in silence. If he has prayed to his Redeemer, he has done so in his cell. He is neither pharisaical nor hypocritical.

"Will you continue in the ministry ?"

Mr. Hayden shook his head. "The disagreement of the jury has, of course, blighted my ministerial prospects," he said. "Nevertheless, the stewards of my church have asked me to return to them. Had a nolle been entered, I might possibly have gone into the pulpit once more, and have felt at liberty to preach. Placed under bonds, my mouth is practically sealed."

"Is the report that you have written an autobiography true ?"

"Yes," he replied. "I have prepared the manuscript while in confinement."

"I have had ill luck," Mr. Hayden said, "in Connecticut. I came here to finish my education. I was taken sick with typhoid fever, and ill luck has attended me ever since. But I have had a few kind friends, and the value of such friends is not appreciated until you are in great trouble. I can never forget those who have stood by me in this hour of trial. I have received many congratulatory letters from strangers in New York and other cities, and you may say that I feel grateful to the writers."

Here Mrs. Hayden and the little boy Lennie entered the cell. The devoted wife had recovered from the strain of the trial. Her face beamed at the prospect of her husband's release. She embraced and kissed him. The boy climbed over the foot of the cot, crying : "I've come to see you, papa." Mr. Hayden caught him in his arms, and both father and mother kissed him repeatedly.

"For thirteen months," said the clergyman, "I did not see my boy. I could not bear to have him brought here." He fondly patted the little head. Lennie is a bright, active urchin, about six years old, and favors his mother in personal appearance. After gazing curiously around the cell, he asked for something to eat.

"Papa's dinner will be brought in directly," said the father, "and Lennie can then eat with papa. Will Lennie sing something for this gentleman ?"

The boy slipped from the little cot to the floor, studied the face of the visitor, and in a low voice sang :

> "Alas! and did my Savior bleed,
> And did my Jesus die ?
> Did he resign his sacred life
> For such a worm as I ?" .

A moment afterward he picked up a rubber band and twisted it over his small fingers while again scrutinizing the face of the stranger. Unconsciously the tune changed. He turned toward the door, singing :

> "Oh, dearest Mae, you're lovelier than the day;
> Your eyes so bright they shine at night,
> When the moon am gone away."

The rubber band dropped to the floor, and he stooped to look for it, but his mother caught him in her arms and passionately fondled him. While running her fingers through his hair she said : "Lennie's hair is too long. It must be cut. Uncle Jesse will take him to the barber."

The little fellow protested on the ground that he did not want to leave papa.

"Oh, papa will soon be home and play with Lennie as he used to do long ago," Mr. Hayden said.

Uncle Jesse arose to depart, and the boy sprang to his father's arms. As he left the cell the visitor gave him a silver coin, suggesting that he might pass a candy store on the way to the barber. Lennie thanked him, saying : "I'll put this with my other money, and I'll soon have enough to pay my way through college."

Mr. and Mrs. Hayden spent several days with their dear friends, Mr. and Mrs. Brownson, in New Haven, and then bade adieu to the many kind people who had stood by with words of cheer in every dark hour. Upon their departure the following appeared in one of the New Haven morning papers :

A CARD.

As the trying scenes of the last sixteen months have reached their crisis, and we are about to leave the city, our hearts swell with gratitude for the many kindnesses received, not only from old and tried friends, but also from those who, up to the time that troubles encompassed us, were to us strangers. The many affectionate tokens of regard, the many kind wishes expressed, will, we are sure, never, never be forgotten. We shall carry with us through life a happy remembrance of those kind offices, and can only say as a parting word, God bless each and every one.

HERBERT H. HAYDEN,
ROSA C. HAYDEN.

New Haven, January 29, 1880.